Douglas Brooke Wheelton Sladen

In Cornwall and Across the Sea

With Poems Written in Devonshire, etc.

Douglas Brooke Wheelton Sladen

In Cornwall and Across the Sea
With Poems Written in Devonshire, etc.

ISBN/EAN: 9783337016975

Printed in Europe, USA, Canada, Australia, Japan

Cover: Foto ©Andreas Hilbeck / pixelio.de

More available books at **www.hansebooks.com**

IN CORNWALL
AND ACROSS THE SEA

WITH POEMS WRITTEN IN DEVONSHIRE

ETC.

BY

DOUGLAS B. W. SLADEN

AN AUSTRALIAN COLONIST

LATE SCHOLAR OF TRINITY COLLEGE, OXFORD ; B.A. OXFORD ;
B.A. AND LL.B. MELBOURNE

AUTHOR OF "FRITHJOF AND INGEBJORG ;" " AUSTRALIAN LYRICS ;"
"A POETRY OF EXILES ;" AND

"A SUMMER CHRISTMAS"

LONDON

GRIFFITH, FARRAN, OKEDEN & WELSH

(SUCCESSORS TO NEWBERY AND HARRIS)

WEST CORNER ST PAUL'S CHURCHYARD

E. P. DUTTON & CO., NEW YORK

1885

TO THE READER.

ALTHOUGH, owing to my absence in the Antipodes, " A Poetry of Exiles " and " A Summer Christmas " appeared in England so lately as last July and last October respectively, they were completed not much less than two years ago. This volume collects the fugitive pieces written during the interval.

The poems entitled " Across the Sea " were written in or of my adopted country—Australia, and my interesting " voyage home," as all Australians patriotically call it, by way of the Indian Ocean and the Mediterranean Sea.

Sonnets 6-19 take the Reader from Ceylon to Plymouth, and were written in sight of the places which they describe. These and the other descriptive sonnets in the volume claim to be photographs

rather than artistic pictures—the function of a photo-
graph being, I take it, to reproduce

" Nature's breadth, yet truth of detail."

My endeavour has been to bring the scenes graphi-
cally before the Reader.

The Poems entitled " In Cornwall " are the fruit
of holidays last autumn spent in that lovely, romantic
and unique county.

The remainder, with few exceptions, were composed
while summering near Bideford or wintering at
Torquay. Those few were composed in London or at
Oxford.

In the schemes of my " Ballades " I have followed
Mr Andrew Lang and Mr Austin Dobson, to whom
I desire here to tender my acknowledgments and
thanks.

DOUGLAS BROOKE WHEELTON SLADEN.

CHERWELL LODGE, OXFORD.
      May, 1885.

TO

THE COUNTESS OF PORTSMOUTH.

IN MEMORY OF PLEASANT HOURS AT EGGESFORD,

THIS BOOK IS,

WITH HER PERMISSION,

𝔇𝔢𝔡𝔦𝔠𝔞𝔱𝔢𝔡.

AT EGGESFORD, EASTER 1885.

OUTSIDE the Hall the Primrose clusters wild,
  Unhid wild Violets rear their lowly heads—
  Each wanton hand that plucks and foot that treads
By the broad shadow of the Hall exiled.

Outside the Hall the Cottar's wife and child
  Can sleep as safely in their lowly beds,
  By the kind Presence, from the Hall which spreads,
From want and trampling force kept undefiled.

Inside the Hall the Spirit, which protects,
  The humble folk and flowers at the gate,
  Pours forth a primrose-violet hue of home,—
Mixed bright and modest,—though it ne'er neglects
  The higher living meet for high estate,
  The duties which with lofty lineage come.

INDEX.

ADDENDA.

PART I.

IN CORNWALL.

A

ALICE OF THE LEA.

(Founded upon a Legend Related by the
Rev. R. S. Hawker.)

In the castle of the Grenvilles
Beside the Cornish sea,
There was to be a wassail
And dance and revelrie,
And who should be the fairest
But Alice of the Lea?

With eyes as blue as heaven
When summer days are bright,
And like "the summer waters
When the sea is soft with light,"
But tresses like the raven,
On murk December night.

As graceful as the ash-tree
　　Down in her native west,
As stately as Tintagel,
　　With castle-cinctured crest,
In all the bounds of Cornwall,
　　Of all the maids the best.

The daring knights of Devon
　　And squires of Cornish strand,
And lords from o'er the Severn Sea
　　Came courting for her hand.
But she loved the lordly Grenvilles
　　Alone of all the land.

And who of all the Grenvilles
　　The maiden's heart should move?
Sir Bevil, the king's captain,
　　Who with the Roundheads strove,
Who battled like a hero
　　And died as heroes love.

But Bevil, the king's captain,
  He thought not of the maid,
Who all her tender girlhood
  And stately beauty laid
Before him, in rich sacrifice,
  And little heed he paid.

In the castle of the Grenvilles
  Beside the Cornish Sea,
They gathered for a wassail
  And dance and revelrie,
And who should be the fairest
  But Alice of the Lea?

But what availed it Alice
  Though queen of all were she
If the proud heart of the Grenville
  Should still unaltered be—
The peerless Lady Alice
  Lady Alice of the Lea?

"O mother and my maidens,
My velvet to me bring,
My gown of the black velvet—
Fit fabric for a king ;
And from my jewel-casket
Give out the pixies' ring—

"The ring won from the pixies
By a wise wife of the Lea—
The mightiest in magic
Of all the West-countree?
To give the love of her true love
Whoever he might be."

But, because the ring was given
Against the pixies' will,
It never won a lover
Without a dower of ill,
And whenever lady wore it
There was thunder in the hill.

"O Alice, daughter Alice,
  Wear not that ring to-night,
For whoso wears that jewel
  Defies the pixies' might,
And to-night the pixies are abroad
  From dusk to dawn of light.

" O Alice, daughter Alice,
  I pray thee set it by ;
When thou art in thy velvet,
  No queen with thee may vie
For stately grace and lovely face
  And glamour of the eye.

"O Alice, daughter Alice,
  The ladies of the Lea
Have jewels of their own enow
  Without the pixies' fee ;
I prayed thee then, I pray thee now,
  To let that jewel be.

"O Alice, daughter Alice,
    I would see thee fairly wed,
And comely children by thee
    Before that I am dead,
By thine own royal beauty
    Not by the pixies sped."

But the lovely lady Alice,
    The lady of the Lea,
Answered her weeping mother,
    Proudly and scornfully,
"I will wear the ring and win his love
    Whatever knight it be."

Then did she on her velvet
    (Fit fabric for a king),
And on her slender finger
    She drew the pixies' ring,
And then looked on her beauty
    In the mirror glorying.

"O Alice, daughter Alice,
　　There is thunder in the hill,
And I feel a brooding boding,
　　In mine inmost soul, of ill ;
I pray thee, daughter mine, to pray,
　　If wear this ring thou will.

"And I pray to Him in heaven
　　That thou mayest win the love
Of him, whose heart thou settest
　　Thy mother's prayers above,
And pray thou win not harm, like all
　　Who pixies' power would prove."

She gazed into the mirror
　　Upon her loveliness,
And on the flashing jewel
　　And her rich velvet dress,
And felt a glow of conscious pride
　　Through her whole being press.

And she gazed into the mirror
　Upon her glorious eyes,
And she muttered, " Pray, or pray not,
　Not Sir Bevil can despise
The glitter and the glamour
　Which all my lovers prize.

" I will not pray, my mother,
　For surely he must yield
To mine own beauty had I
　No pixies' ring to wield ;
Nor care I for the pixies aught,
　In hall or in the field.

" I will not pray, my mother ;
　There's little done by pray'r
But may be done by woman's face
　Or man's right arm, or care ;
The pixies I defy to do
　Whatever they may dare.

Forthwith there shone a glare of light
　Which dazzled all the place,
But when the glare had vanished
　None saw the maiden's face,
Although they scoured the country side
　For twelve long hours' space,

And in the Grenvilles' castle
　Beside the Cornish Sea
There was a gloom of sorrow,
　For the fairest, where was she,
The queen of all who graced each ball.
　The lady of the Lea?

But when the news was brought them
　They hasted, one and all,
Bedizened in the splendour
　Done on them for the ball,
To scour the manor of the Lea
　And search the ancient hall,—

The daring knights of Devon
　And squires of Cornish strand,
And lords from o'er the Severn Sea
　Who sought the maiden's hand.
And Bevil whom the maiden loved
　Alone of all the land.

But never spied the maiden
　Even a moment's space,
And they sorrowed, some for years,
　O'er the beauty of her face,
And Bevil for her evil hap,
　But no whit for her grace ;

Though he, alone, of all men
　The maiden's heart might move,
But in a score of battles
　Against the Roundheads strove,
And bore him like a hero,
　And died as heroes love.

Only the pixies' jewel
   Beneath the earth was found,
Laid lightly near the surface
   Of a mole's new-built mound—
The first of all the molehills
   Cast up on Cornish ground.

And the simple country people
   Said that the little mole,
With her fur like rich black velvet
   And her eye with hidden hole,
Was the lost and scornful maiden
   Whom the angry pixies stole,

With fur of rich black velvet,
   Like the robe which she had worn,
And the eyes she was so proud of
   That prayer she should scorn,
As a judgment for vain-glory,
   Out of their sockets torn.

And they say that at the seasons
When pixies feast and jest,
She regains her shape and beauty
And is their honoured guest,
As honest folks have witnessed
In the borders of the West.

THF BELLS OF FORRABURY.

(Founded upon a Legend related by the Rev. R. S. Hawker.)

The Lord of Bottreaux Castle,
 Was of all men haughtiest,
He could not brook the waft of bells
 Borne on the breeze's breast
From the church-tower of Tintagel
 When the wind blew from the west.

And he charged a famous founder,
 Who lived in London town,
To cast a peal of bells to be
 A glory and renown
To the tower of Forrabury
 Upon the windy down.

The founder in his foundry,
　　Great bells he founded three
The first was for St Michael named,
　　For merciful is he
To shipwrecked folk and strangers
　　Upon the land or sea;

The second was named after
　　The sons of Zebedee,
Because that they were fishermen
　　In far off Galilee;
And the third for Mother Mary
　　And the infant at her knee.

The bells were wrought and graven
　　And carried to be blest,
With holy water, hand and voice
　　By bishop, choir and priest,
Then put upon the vessel
　　To bear into the west.

The Bells of Forrabury.

The west wind blew them fairly
    From London to the sea :
The east wind sped the good ship on
    Till past the land was she :
And then the west wind took them
    And bore them merrily,

Until they cast their anchor
    Right under Willapark,
Not daring, till the tide was in
    And dawn had chased the dark,
To thread the tortuous harbour
    With their rich-laden bark.

The Vespers of Tintagel
    Once more resounded clear ;
But filled they not the Bottreaux folk
    With envy now but cheer,
For the bells had come to Bottreaux
    After so many a year.

B

The Vespers of Tintagel
    Were wafted to the sea ;
The Pilot crossed himself and dropped
    Down on his bended knee,
And for safe voyage and speedy
    His thanksgiving breathed he.

"What dost thou, Master Pilot,
    Upon thy bended knee?
What words are those thou mutterest,
    I prythee, tell to me?"
"I am praising Mother Mary
    For her mercies on the sea."

" Fie on thee, Master Pilot,
    Are we not good enow,
On summer-seas as soft as these
    To bring to port our bow ?
Thy captain and his seamen,
    Not saints, should have thy vow.

" Fie on thee, Master Pilot !"
   And a dread oath he swore,
That he could save his ship alone
   Though all the winds did roar
And all the saints in heaven
   Should keep him from the shore.

The pilot bowed him meekly
   And turned to heaven once more,
That God the captain might forgive
   For the dread oath he swore,
And no ill hap might take them
   Ere they should reach the shore.

When the red sunset gilded
   The castle of Bottreaux,
The sea was like a little lake,
   Where never ripples flow,
By wooded banks veiled closely
   From all the winds that blow :

When rose the moon, the waters
　　Shone like a mirror-glass,
Not clear but lined with silver sheen,
　　Where all things that may pass
Cast shadows on its surface
　　Like breath on polished brass.

The waters lapped as gently
　　Upon the headland's crags
As a deep sluggish-river tide,
　　Wherein the reedy flags
Move little, as the watchful pike
　　Who in their arbours lags.

The torch-fire in the cresset
　　Rose straight, a shaft of flame,
Steady as light of well-trimmed wick
　　When shielded by a frame
Of graven glass pourtraying
　　Some deed of ancient fame.

"Go sleep thee, whining pilot,"
  The scornful captain said,
" Thou needst no crossings, bended knees
  Or beads to save thy head :
Thou art as safe on shipboard
  To-night as in thy bed."

" I will not sleep, Sir Captain,
  I will not sleep to-night :
We shall be safe by grace of heaven,
  When morning brings the light :
Who stays his hand in battle,
  Not often wins the fight."

But went that scornful captain
  And laid him down to sleep,
As careless in his fragile bark
  Upon the vengeful deep,
As the lord of Bottreaux Castle
  In his mighty feudal keep.

But while the scornful captain
　And all his seamen slept,
A great wave, in mid-ocean born,
　Of storm or earthquake, swept
And on the fated vessel
　Like a huge serpent leapt.

And, fettered with her anchors,
　The gallant little bark
Was strangled in the serpent's folds,
　Right under Willapark,
In the hour before the morning,
　The hour of all most dark.

But the prayerful pilot standing
　At his post upon the deck,
Was borne in safety to the land
　Upon the monster's neck,
While the captain and the seamen
　Were strangled in the wreck.

And rising in the morning,
 The vassals of Bottreaux
Looked for the ship which bore their bells,
 But saw a sight of woe,
The shipwrecked pilot wailing
 The stout ship whelmed below.

" Tell us, thou mournful seaman,
 What mournest thou ?" they said,
" Or hast thou lost thy boat or nets ?
 Or is some comrade dead ?
Or tell us art thou shipwrecked
 And all thy substance sped ? "

Then spoke the pilot wailing,
 "Shipwrecked I am," he said,
" But mourn not only boat or net,
 Or trusty comrade dead ;
For the bells of Bottreaux church-tower
 Swing on the ocean's bed.

Long centuries are over
  Since the good ship went down,
With Forrabury's bells on board,
  In sight of Bottreaux town,
Yet the "silent tower of Bottreaux"
  No chime hath ever known.

But the bells of Forrabury
  Give forth a muffled knell,
From their belfry in the sunken ship,
  The danger to foretell,
When from the far Atlantic
  There strides a sudden swell.

And the fishers of the haven,
  Though smooth as glass the sea,
And though the heavens overheard
  From rack or cloud are free,
Though breeze enough there is not
  A signal flag to see,

If they think they hear the knelling
    Of the Forrabury bells,
Say 'tis the scornful captain who
    A coming storm foretells,
And he his boat who launches
    Hears his own funeral knells.

But the bells of high Tintagel
    Still merrily ring on,
As, long ere Norman William came,
    They haughtily have done,
While the bells of Forrabury
    Were not, have come, have gone.

ST IVES, CORNWALL.

THE day that I wandered down to St Ives
I saw no man with a number of wives,
Or cats or anything else of the kind
Of which the old legend put me in mind,

But only the town with its quaint old streets
And the quaint old quay with its fisher fleets
And sunburnt fishermen watching the tide
Or drying their nets on the Island side,

And fisherwomen hard-worked but gay
For fine it was nor the boats away,
And sturdy children some swimming about
Some bare on the sand when the tide was out.

When the tide was out there was gleaming sand
Stretching leagues away upon either hand,
Dividing the dark blue sea and the shore
With its crown of boulder and heathy moor.

There's little to laugh at about St Ives :
Its story's a serious story of lives
Nightly in risk on the pitiless sea
To earn the fisher's inadequate fee,

A story of lifeboat, rocket and belt,
A story of woe not talked of but felt
When a lugger puts out to sea and goes
The way which all know of but no one knows.

Good-bye, little town by the Severn sea
With your sands and old inns and your busy quay,
And your carven church and your antique streets,
And your sun-burned heroes of fisher fleets !

Good-bye ! when I read the name of St Ives
The wives I shall think of are fishermen's wives,
Rearing their sons to be heroes at home
While the wild wind lashes the western foam

Round the boats, in which brothers and husbands sail,
To win their bread from the teeth of the gale,
Or to carry a chance of life to wrecks
At the risk of their own stout hearts and necks.

THE MERMAID OF ZENNOR—A BALLAD.

O STRANGERS from Australia,
   And strangers born at home,
Who know no more of England
   Than those from o'er the foam,

There is a church at Zennor,
   By the North Cornish sea,
Where our forefathers worshipped
   And worship still may we

In an old-fashioned building,
   In the old-fashioned style;
The church has still a Saxon floor
   And early-English aisle.

The carving of the chancel
 Is plaster-overlaid ;
'Twas done two centuries ago
 When sturdy Roundheads prayed.

But the bench ends carved grotesquely
 Of honest English oak
Have all, save two, departed,
 In the common way of folk.

And these two are Zennor's glory,
 More especially the one
With the figure of a mermaid
 Rudely and oldly done.

Why the figure of a mermaid
 Should grace a Christian church
Has defied whole generations
 Of original research.

But we know no better reason
  Than the Zennor people told,
In the days when men believed things,
  In the fairy days of old.

For the squire's son of Zennor,
  So the ancient legend said,
Sang so sweetly that he drew to land
  A wondering sea-maid,

Who loved him and allured him
  Down to her ocean home,
To go and be a merman
  Beneath Atlantic foam.

And they never saw him after
  And carved the maid in oak
To show how she was fashioned,
  Who lured him from his folk.

For of all the men in Cornwall
    There are none can sing a glee
Like the singing men of Zennor
    Beside the Severn sea.

But the neighbours say the reason
    Why the maid was carved in oak
Was because a heathen mermaid
    Had taught the Zennor folk.

And the parson said the mermaid
    Was a figure of the sea,
Because the first apostles
    Had fished in Galilee.

Well—anyhow the mermaid
    Is carved in heart of oak,
And Zennor men sing better
    Than any other folk—
So Zennor people tell you,
    In earnest or in joke.

THE CAPTIVE RIVER.

AN IDYLL OF THE CORNISH MINES.

I SPRANG to life upon the heights,
   Which frown on Zennor and the ocean.
A fairy, born for daring flights
   From rock to rock, for wayward motion
'Twixt overarching banks of heather
   On the wild moorlands of my birth,
A mate for gossamer or feather
   Almost too pure a thing for earth.

Impatient of my tardy growth,
    I hastened down toward the valley,
Like many, who repent it, loath
    In childhood's fairyland to dally.
I grew, with gifts of tribute waters
    By humbler sister fairies brought,
Until, of all the mountain's daughters
    The greatest, I the lowlands sought.

I scorned my soft brown moorland bed,
    I scorned the gleaming floor of gravel,
Which stained my feet not, as I sped
    Upon my downward path of travel.
I longed to show a crowded city
    My pure, wild beauty, knowing not
That hunger's victims cannot pity
    Or praise, but only bruise and blot.

In quest of praise in peopled lands
I gained a little mining village,
Only, with my free limbs in bands,
To find myself constrained to pillage
The bright ore from the mountain bower
Where it and I were born, and drive
The mighty wheel that yields the power
Which animates the busy hive.

Freed from the wheel I hoped in vain
Once more at my caprice to ramble,
To cross the open moors again
Amid the heather, brake and bramble.
In vain, still captive, was I hurried
'Twixt narrow wooden walls to find,
When I emerged befoamed and flurried,
Only some other wheel to grind.

At last, my captors I escaped,
  Only to find the wished-for city,
Through which my passage now I shaped,
  A sight to move my wrath and pity.
My banks were void of leaf or flower,
  My path as closely straitened in
With vice and want in all their power,
  With views of strife and smoke and sin.

My only hope was now the sea,
  The pure, untainted, fragrant ocean.
Might not to mingle waters be
  A cleansing, health-restoring potion?
Were not the Cornish sands a-sparkle,
  The Cornish seas of that rare hue,
Which, as they grow alight or darkle,
  Varies from beryl-green to blue?

Alas ! the seas and sands were bright,
    Until the mountain's fairy daughter
Defiled their pureness, quenched their light,
    By contact with her sullied water.
Stained was I, with my violence, ruddy
    When I the mountain's wealth out-forced ;
And now the very seas turned bloody,
    Fouled by my touch, where'er I coursed.

O welcome, welcome, open sea !
    O welcome, welcome, stormy ocean !
Though lost in your wide arms I be,
    Lost is my stain in your commotion.
My feet upon the moor are spotless,
    But I my guilty head must hide,
No matter where, so it be blotless,
    And what I plunge it in be wide.

SIR TRISTRAM AT TINTAGEL.

Written after a Visit to Tintagel in Aug. 1884.

Ysolde.

Sir Tristram back? O wherefore art thou here?
The King will slay thee, and an outlawed man
Breaking his ten years' parol, as thou dost,
The Barons dare not shield thee.

Tristram.

                    But, O Queen,
The King himself released me, holding me
Hard-fastened by the hand. With him I came.

Ysolde.

The King?

TRISTRAM.

The King, for haled to Arthur's Court,

A yielded recreant, by Launcelot

And there appeached of treason on a Knight,

Sir Bersules, cleaving him unawares,

And for no cause but that he would not aid

In compassing my treasonable death,

Arthur, as penance, bade him join accord

And pass with me to ride into his realm.

YSOLDE.

Sir Tristram, trust him not !   He is my lord,

God knows to my dishonour and sore pain—

And well I know that in his shrewd black heart,

Full of foul treason, hate and subtle guile,

With thee he never truly will accord.

He hates thee first for thy well-favouredness,

Being himself ill-favoured—more than that

For good which thou hast wrought him, winning him

His crown of Cornwall and deliverance

From tribute to my father, and for praise

The people give thee, calling thee the grace

And mirrour of all knighthood in the west,

Here and in Lyonesse and most of all—

Ah me that I confess it—for my love

Which thou hast won from him—nay thou hast held

From the beginning thine in his despite.

Oh ! Tristram, he will slay thee, when thy limbs

Are fast in bands laid treacherously on,

Or smite thee through the back, or set on thee

One man unarmed with half a score of Knights.

TRISTRAM.

Fear not, great heart, I fear not !

YSOLDE.

Tristram, heed !

Behold this rock we stand on how immense,

Towering aloft, joined to the Cornish hills

With rocky wall so thick that chariots

Might pass upon its brow, and yet leave space

For rows of other chariots to stand

On either side where the two chariots passed.

See yon black pool beneath us, 'tis not great

And it is far below, and yet that pool

Little by little in the course of time

Our rock will sever (rock) from the friendly shore,

And maybe afterwards o'erwhelm the rock,

Or strip it of the fabric fair, which crowns

Its stately head.—Mayhap, where we two stand,

In after days, but a low ruinous wall

Or crumbling bank shall show the royal hill

From any desert tor upon the moors.

Mark is the pool tireless and deep and black,

And far below thee as it lies below.

Thou art the stately promontory joined

To the whole land of Cornwall in men's hearts.

But as beneath this—even now—are caves

Sapped by the sea, through which on stormy nights

The breakers with low ominous thunder roar,

So there are signs.

See Tristram, here is samphire,

Which grows not but on sheer sea-beaten cliffs.

This samphire with its golden flowers and leaves,

So gentle to soft touch, but being bruised,

So pungent is for thee and Launcelot

To wear upon your casques, you two who stand

Like island-cliffs for wind and wave to lash.

O Tristram, thou and Launcelot : but nay,

I must not talk of Launcelot and thee ;

For folk will think of me and Guinevere,

Twin Queens disloyal—yet we had our loves

Before our Lords.   Did I not give my love,

Tristram, to thee for ever ?   It was lent,

But for a while, to Mark at thy behest ;

And being thine, thou mayest call it back

At thy good pleasure.   Tristram, mindest thou,

When we were yet in Ireland and unwed ?

And how I healed thee of thy grievous hurt?

And how I hated Sir Palamides,

And gave thee the white armour, which thou worest

When thou so greatly overthrewest him—

White armour from a maid to maiden Knight?

Our hearts were white then, white had they been now

Had we but kept them true unto themselves,—

Nay! they are white; for a great love, once given

And never faltered from, must needs be white;

And we have never faltered in our love,

Although obedience and circumstance

Have crossed the hands, which should have only met.

    Oh Tristram, I should bid thee hold thine arm

From round my body, and forbear my lips.

What would men say who saw the imperious Queen,

Ysolde the proud, Ysolde the stern and high,

The dark repellant Ysolde, yielding her,

To love's caresses like a budding girl

Who hath not lost the lesson of the child

Though she hath learned the lore of womanhood?

And yet I cannot bid thee. Child I am

With thee: for hast thou not the countersign

To take thee past each line of my defence

Right to the keep?   I have no gate for thee,

No watch, no ward.   Nay! Kiss me not again !

Thy kisses are thy Queen's—the fair Ysolde's,

The lily-fingered Ysolde's.   O my love

Why didst thou wed this beautiful Ysolde,

This chaste, this sweet unquestioning Ysolde,

This noble Ysolde, asking thee for nought

But giving thee her all, thy children's mother,

Upbraiding not for absence, nor for love

Pre-mortgaged to another, and forespent,

And me thereby upbraiding ten times more

Than if she heaped ten thousand curses on me ?

Thinkest thou if I loved Mark—impossible !—

But if I could, that I would have his love,

His time, his thoughts, his presence, everything

Wasted upon an old discarded love ?

Nay, Tristram, by " discarded " I mean nought,

No querulousness ; but, when I think on her,

I can but sigh for that which might have been

If thou hadst not obeyed thine uncle-king

So loyally, when he demanded me,

Nor I fulfilled my word so loyally,

Which unto thee I sware that I would wed

Whomso thou wishedst, deeming if not thee

'Twere somewhat to have wed thy chosen friend.

Had we not been so childish-loyal then,

We had been loyaller now.   Oh ! 'tis a sin

To bind oneself to fealty, which leaves

No choice but wrong or disobedience.

And as with me so with Queen Guinevere :

I cannot but compare myself with her,

A king's wife, as I am, so royally loved

And honoured and dishonoured by that love.

TRISTRAM.

Nay, Ysolde, I am liker her than thou,

For she hath wed the gentlest Knight alive

And I the gentlest maid.   And Launcelot,

He never had a lover but the Queen,

Or thou but me.   For Mark was not thy love

But my behest.   I am like Guinevere

And Launcelot the truest Knight alive,

Who ever bears his great love for the Queen

Between him and all maids.—What greater love

Can any cherish than to stay unwed,

Because the woman of his love is wed,

And wait upon the lady of his love,

By day and night, when be it that he may,

To do her what true service he may chance ?

YSOLDE.

And thou, O Tristram, what dost thou but this ?

TRISTRAM.

Nay, sweet, I did not so as Launcelot

But wedded me.

YSOLDE.

                    O Tristram, blame to me

That ever I was wed.   Why did not I,

Failing thy choice of me to be thy wife,

Go out to be a handmaid to thy wife,

I the proud Ysolde, I the stern and high

Whom men, for my unbending spirit dread

As more than woman, shun as one possessed?

Oh! how I would that I were with thy wife

As chamber-woman, menial—what not,—

To be about thee alway, and to smooth

Thy life with faithful service vigilant,

And yet not take thee from her.   She hath won

Upon me with her gentleness so well

That I could spare her any grace but one—

Thy presence.   Were I by, she might be Queen.

  Oh! how I hate Tintagel!   Its huge cliffs,

Black pools and wrathful waves are ominous

Of wild, precipitous, storm-beaten lives.

The place is fraught with magic and with storm;

Merlin bewitched it—here another Queen

Was loved by one—not her own Lord—too well;

And here was found a little naked babe—

Her babe say some and some say Gothlois—

Which brought by the enchanter and bred up,

Hath grown to be the source of many battles,

Albeit it grew to be the blameless king.

Nor do I think this rock will e'er be blest

Or any castle long will stand thereon

Though many there be built.

TRISTRAM.

Nay, fear not, sweet !

We shall spend many golden days herein,

On velvet turf reposing with the breeze

Fresh blowing from the west to feed our lungs,

With the rich Cornish sun to mellow us,

And league-long cliffs to gaze at, and blue seas

Surf-crested by the reefs with fringe of foam,

And sough or roar of waves to lull our ears,

And ferns for me to gather from sea-caves

To deck thy glossy hair.   The king-seal's fur

Shall wrap thy slim form from the winter's blast,

For am I not renowned the hunter-knight ?

And I will hear thee harp with that same touch

I taught thee when thou satest on my knee,

In Ireland as thou healed'st me of my hurt,

Rewarding thee with kisses, little one,

For thou wast little then in years, though grown

Into a budding wealth of womanhood.

And we will ride and hawk upon the hills

And chase the swift red stag upon the moors

And—

YSOLDE.

Nay, my love, but, Mark !

TRISTRAM.

I fear not Mark.

YSOLDE.

Nor I, in field ; but Mark is treacherous

And full of wiles, face-friendly, unrelaxed,

Relentless, unforgetting.

TRISTRAM.

He hath sworn.

D

YSOLDE.

A thousand times, but when kept he an oath
Longer than he had need to save his skin
From present peril.   Mark will not forgive.

TRISTRAM.

But—

YSOLDE.

But what?

TRISTRAM.

But Mark will not forget,
And Launcelot hath sworn upon his head
To visit treason done in my despite
On Mark's own head, though heaven and earth shall
fall.

CORNISH SONNETS.

CORNWALL.

CORNWALL, thou rivallest the border-land

  In the romance, which thrills the poet's heart:

  Indeed a border-land thyself thou art,

Where British Douglases did stoutly stand

'Gainst Saxon Percies—wouldest have as grand

  A roll of ballad-heroes on thy part

  If only the true tale of what thou wert

Had not been blurred with Time's obscuring hand

  In the long centuries, like the granite stone

    On tombs in thine old churchyards.   Lyonnesse,

  Tintagel, maybe Camelot, are thine own:

    And on thine uplands lingered the impress

  Of pixy, giant, exorcist so long

  That still they leaven cottage tale and song.

II.

Nor hast thou only legend and romance :
 For does not dusty board, in wayside fane,
 Oft to the antiquary's search make plain
How stoutly Cornish halberds did advance
King Charles's cause ?   And where could artist glance
 On boulders like Treen's Castle-of-the-Dane,
 Or mightier billows rolling from the main
Than those which hurl their winter puissance
 Against Tintagel and the Land's-end cliffs,
  While from the dim recesses of thine heart
 The stream of wealth has risen, since the skiffs
  Of the Phœnicians took that to the mart
 Which gave those islands of the northern seas
 Their ancient name of *Cassiterides.*

SONNETS ON THE CORNISH MOORS.

ON THE CORNISH MOORS.

HE, whom the Muse beguiles, doth seldom note
　　The flight of time or covering of space,
　　But rambles on with absent-minded face,
Oft with light tread, though blistered be his foot
His body weary and his goal remote ;
　　The mind's impatience wearies more than pace ;
　　And he who feeds or lulls his mind, can brace
A weary frame to task too heavy put.
　　I had been climbing all a summer day :
　　　　Over rough Cornish moors had been my roam :
　　　　Jaded and footsore was I, far from home.
　　And thrice as far it seemed to lie away,
　　　　When suddenly the Muse spoke, and I sped
　　　　As lightly home as though enchantment-led.

II.

The Cornish moors ! what visions raise they not
　Of fairies, pixies, giants, knights, and kings?
　For here the latest fairies danced their rings
And pixies lurked in every lonely spot
To lure the traveller : and giants wrote
　Their history in stones whose vastness sings,
　As never minstrel might who harped on strings,
The giants' mighty lives.　Here Tristram smote
　In his first fight, and Arthur in his last
　　Beside the slaughterous bridge of Camelford
After the power of his knights had passed,
　　And here the loyal Cornishmen have poured
Times out of mind their blood in any cause
Which seemed to simple folk for Nature's laws.

CASTLE CHUN.

I.

A MIGHTY ring of granite stones, unhewn,
  Like beaches raised by the Atlantic tide
  On Cornish coasts, a brambled moat outside,
And, bounding that, a giant's wall—half strewn,
Half indestructible—are Castle Chûn.
  Within it is one carpet, fairy-dyed,
  Of heather-crimson and gorse-gold allied,
Fern-fringed with green.   Late on an afternoon
  We scaled the castle-hill : the sun had gone,
    But on the ruins of long-vanished pride
  The haze of the departed godhead shone,
    So lately 'neath horizon did he glide.
  Was it not meet?   His rays would have revealed
  The ravages his haze did fondly shield.

II.

Glorious it were to spend a summer night,—

    A sweet soft night in June,—within these walls,

    Listening to distant owl and curlew calls,

And conjuring up a vision of the fight,

Which strewed the moor, a cloth-yard arrow's flight,

    With barrow, cist, and cromlech.   What appals

    The ignorant and timid only thralls

The lover of the mystic with delight.

    Giant or fay were no unwelcome guest,

        Or ghost of Norseman, or Round-Table knight

    Still of the phantom Sangreal in quest.

        If such there came, might not there come a sight

    Of the huge castle in its ancient pride,—

    High-walled, deep-moated, and with kings inside?

Castle Chun.

It weighs but little in the poet's mind
    By whom 'twas reared—the dark Euskarian
    (Who named us " Britons," our primæval man,)
Against the Celt, or by the Celt designed
To stay the Teuton conqueror and find
    Brief respite from the Viking. If blood ran
    In great old battles, if for long months' span
'Twas resolutely held, when hope had pined,
    And food had wasted, it is haunted ground ;
      Even if a bandit, preying on his kind,
    In these stupendous stones a fastness found.
      It matters not who stone to stone doth bind.
    Castles we love as stages where great plays
    By famous men were acted in old days.

RIALOBRAN, THE SON OF CUNOVAL.

RIALOBRAN, the Son of Cunoval,
  This is inscribed in Latin on a stone,
  Rough hewn and rudely lettered, standing lone
Beneath Carn Galva.   Was he general
Or hero ?   Did he valiantly fall
  Fighting the Saxon ?   Did wild women moan
  Over a bulwark of the people gone ?
Why shared he not the common fate of all,
  Who lived and died and were forgotten here,
    That his one stone the moors of Penwith hold,
  Gay-gardened at the season of the year
    With bramble-fruit, heath-purple, and gorse-gold,
  And with two castles of his ancient race
  Guarding in ruined pride his burial place.

SONNETS OF MOUNTS BAY.

PENZANCE.

PENZANCE, I gazed upon you many a time
  Across the bay: now tropically blue,
  Now white with wrath and threatening to strew
Ship and sea-wall in common wreck sublime.
I gazed upon you when the morning prime
  Gilt tower and dome, and when the summer threw
  A veil of mist and splendour over you
As seven of the even rang its chime.
  In pensive mood I gazed upon your lights
    Guiding the pilchard-fisher through the gloom,
    When I threw up the window of my room
  For the cool breeze on fine September nights,
    And hope for many a pleasant ramble still
    Through your quaint streets or up Lescudjack's
      hill.

MOUNT'S BAY.

SEPTEMBER 6TH, 1884.

THE storm had passed, the breakers died away,

The setting sun, a crown of glory, pressed

On ocean's sinking head, while from the west

A fresh wind blew, no longer fierce but gay.

One ray illumed St Michael's Mount, one ray

The Land's last range, and one the meadowy nest

Beneath the leas of Ludgvan, and the rest

The foaming locks of ocean tossed and grey.

I called the legend to my mind, which told

That round the Mount for miles a forest grew,

Where sands have blown, meads bloomed, and

waters rolled,

For centuries; and could not deem it true,

Had not the workmen, digging in the ground

Two fathoms deep, the ancient forest found.

MARAZION.

SEPTEMBER 14TH, 1884.

THE day was warm, as many an Austral day,
  And all day the September sun had rained
  On sand and old seawall rough-weather-stained
And on the tide-filled waters of the bay
So pitilessly that the idler lay
  In each chance shadow, or if he had gained
  The friendly shelter of a house, remained
Until the storm of heat had passed away.
  Yet, ere the sun waned, when the tide ran down
    And I the causeway to the Mount had crossed
      In search of cool, the East wind blew so cold
  That I remembered winter days I'd known
    In New South Wales with scorch at noon but frost
      At eve, like strong men suddenly grown old.

ST MICHAEL'S MOUNT.

SEPTEMBER 25TH, 1884.

St Michael's Mount ! four weeks did I abide
    Beneath its shadow ; yet I entered not
    Its castle though I haunted the wild spot
Moated with ocean every flush of tide.
Oft was I tempted sore to pass inside ;
    It seemed so heedless, when it was one's lot
    To be so near, to miss it, and I wot
That I enjoy the oft-derided pride
    Of seeing all the wonders of the earth,
        As wonders, though 'twere but a fleeting glance.
    Yet what was vain inquisitiveness worth
        When put into the scales with the romance,
    Which I could weave about each ancient wall,
    While distance held me in enchantment's thrall ?

II.

While I was shielded from the common round
  And commonplace of modern social life,
  Piano, Paris-dress and paperknife,
Afternoon tea and tennis, I was crowned
An ancient king, could tread enchanted ground
  With fairy queens, and couch a lance in strife
  With mailed knights-errant. Might not Tristram's
    wife—
Did he not dwell in Lyonnesse's bound?—
  Be in yon tower, or else the Cornish Queen
    For whom he died. And if I heard a fount
Of music from the church, it must have been
    The Norman Fathers from the elder mount.
  Was the hall lit? The valiant cavalier
  Offered the ruined ·Stuart-Queen high cheer.

III.

With dreams and visions of Arturian knight

    And monk from Mont St Michel d'Outremer

    Migrated to the Guarded Mount, the air

Which floated round the castle rock was bright.

Once more the Norman scorning terms and flight

    Opened his resolute veins, and stout De Vere

    Extorted his free pardon.   Then a pair

Of strangely mated lovers met my sight,

    Scotland's white rose, child of an honoured name,

      And he, who born of Flemish chapman, yet

So like to England's royal Edward came

    That Edward's sister had the will to set

The ancient crown of England on his head,

And Scotland gave her choicest flower to wed.

IV.

We know but little of this fair mock-queen
    Left in the castle, while her mock-king went
    To lead the angered Cornish into Kent
And rouse the riversiders, who had been
Foremost, whenever force did intervene
    'Twixt wrong and weakness. When, with marching
        spent,
    His troops were routed, thou wast ta'en and sent
To the crowned King. What was it in thy mien
  That melted that stern heart? how didst thou weep
    And blush thy shame, that he who spared so few
  Should pardon thee and bid his White Rose keep
    This Scottish Rose beside her? Thou hast shared
  The fate of many a flow'r of olden time,
  Whose tale has passed from history to rhyme.

ST MICHAEL'S MOUNT, CORNWALL,
AT SUNSET.

I.

AFTER a burning day, when even came,
   I climbed a cliff which looked across the bay,
   And glanced to where St Michael's Mountain lay
Dissevered by a mirrored shaft of flame,—
As ruddy as a maiden's blush of shame,—
   And a flood-tide with evening shadows grey
   From Marazion.   There I mused away
On Tristram's early praise and later blame,
   And how upon this very rock once stood
     The gleaming castle called through Lyonesse
In Tristram's day, " The White Tower in the wood,"
     While forest, meadow, towns and palaces
   Were bowered from here to Scilly's utmost bound,
   Where long the ocean hath usurped the ground.

II.

I gazed upon the castle of to-day,

At first behind a halo amber-dyed,

Which half-concealed it and half fairified

Until no mortal pencil could convey

The glory of the picture—fit for fay

Or Knight of old romance. I turned aside,

Forgetful that a vision might not bide,

And, when I looked again, the pageant gay

Had vanished and a sorcerer's fastness rose

Black from the precipice,—no aperture

For door or window,—such as Doré shows

With his grim brush, till the sun grew obscure.

And every point of tower and crag did leave

In bold relief with the clear light of eve.

III.

The bay around was placid as a lake,

    And locked with land on every side save one;

    The pilchard boats had, with the setting sun,

Launched out their nightly task to undertake;

Some few small feathered songsters were awake,

    Their evensong of thanksgiving scarce done;

    And to their pastures with their udders run

The cows slow way were wending through the brake.

    Bathed in warm sunset, sate we there until

        The first bleak breeze of even warned us home,

    Fain on the fairy scene to linger still

        But fearful to be caught, while we might roam,

    By the cold outstretched fingers of the night

    Stripping its iris-vesture from the sight.

ST MICHAEL'S MOUNT BY MOONLIGHT.

AT Marazion, I remember well
How that I stood half a September night,
To feast my eyes on the enchanted sight
Exceeding all the poet's art to tell,
St Michael's Mountain with its citadel
Against the moonlit sky outstanding bright,
And long dark headlands stretching left and right
Around the placid bay, that rose and fell,
With soft melodious, incessant sough,
And gently heaving far off lights, which marked
Fishers.   I mused how here the Tyrian
Ages ago adventured and embarked
Tin from this haven, when the Aryan man
Had not emerged from Aryan highlands rough.

TO A YOUNG AUSTRALIAN LADY.

E. M. S.

LADY, I met thee on the Austral shore,
　　Fresh from the very threshold of the grave,
　　And pale as if thou never wouldest have
Health's purple hue and springing footstep more.
A few months passed, and on a ball-room floor
　　Thou glidedst fair and graceful, though too brave.
　　I saw thee then on that side of the wave
No further.　Now upon a Cornish moor
　　Thou standest sunburnt, lithe, and strong of limb
　　　As a young Dian, making the wild heath
　　And fallen cromlechs echo with health's hymn
　　　Of laughter.　Futures who foreshadoweth?
　　How could I dream four years ago of thee
　　Robust, and on these far off hills with me?

SONNETS OF THE LAND'S END.

THE LAND'S END.

I.

THE Land's End is it? with calm beryl sea
   Stretching before me for a score of miles
   To the low, distant, broken rim of isles?
The Land's End pictured in my reverie
Had been a wall of granite on the lee
   Of waves, that mimicked mountains and defiles,
   And flung themselves upon the giant piles
Of boulders, swooping irresistibly,
   Like eagles driving through a wild swan's back
      Their greedy talons deep. Was Lyonnesse
Submerged beneath this sleeping, gleaming track?
      Here was it one alone escaped the stress
Of wind and wave, when o'er Sir Tristram's realm
The angry ocean rushed to overwhelm?

II.

But stay !   Where'er an islet rock appears,
  Where the "Armed Knight" stands sentry o'er
    the strait,
  And fabled "Irish lady" met her fate,
Where the "Long Ships" their warning light uprear,
And the dark "Brisons" rise, cliff-castled sheer,
  A prison for a giant, springs a spate
  Of frosted, seething foam beneath the weight
Of every pounding wave.   It leaps up clear,
  (Like a white ostrich feather shot in air,
    Or like a sunny fountain in the court
  Of palace old) falls, ripples everywhere
    Hissing, then drains straight back with respite
      short,
  Islanding each projecting jag of rock,
  To break or merge in the next billow's shock.

SENNEN—THE VILLAGE UPON THE

LAND'S END.

I.

SENNEN, mere hamlet—with a tiny fane,

  A tavern and farmhouses, what is here

  That pilgrims thread in hundreds year by year

Through the long village past the Table-maen

And roadside-cross? it is that they would gain

  The end of England's land, and gaze down sheer

  From her last cliffs on billows running clear,

Without a barrier, from the Spanish Main.

Majestic is the sight, which strikes the eye,

    Whether the sea is calm—of that rare hue

    Greener than sapphire, more than beryl blue,

  Which gleams in Cornish coves—or threats the sky

With waves that o'er the cliff tops leap on high

    And rend the rocks, and sand with wreckage strew.

II.

Nor is the little cove next Whitesand bay,
   With shelving slide of granite carried down
   Below low-water from the Fishers' Town,
Without its history.   For in his day
After the crowning slaughter at Boleit,
   King Athelstan, to wear his English crown
   E'en to the utmost isles, from hence was blown
By cruel east winds to the lands which lay
   A few leagues off, a bulwark from the west.
      Here later Stephen landed for a throne,
      And coming from his Irish wars King John ;
   And here, in her extremity, sore-pressed,
   She who, of proudest Scottish birth possessed,
      Linked the pretender's fortunes to her own.

III.

White Rose of Scotland, be thy slumber sweet,

 Who, after thy *roi-faineant* was ta'en,

 Taken thyself on Michael's Mount, didst gain

The favour of all eyes which thou didst meet,

Up to cold Henry on his judgment seat,

 From whom with blushes and thine eyes' soft rain,

 Thou, sole of all his captives, didst obtain

Life-mercy. Was thy girlhood so replete

With all which sweetens and illumines life,

  That thou thy forfeit neck couldst lightly win

  From these stern men not slow to slay their kin.

In the long years of internecine strife

That followed on the baring of the knife

  Which finished the two Roses' council-din.

VELLANDREATH—WHITESAND BAY.

BY Whitesand Bay report beholds at night
  The spirits of the folk who have been drowned
  In what was ancient Lyonnesse's bound,
And fisher-folk still shrink in strange affright
From treading on its shores before the light
  Or after dusk.   Why this is haunted ground
  We know not if 'tis not that here are found,
The corpses which have foundered in the bight,
  After the storm blows over.   Once we know
    The cruel Spaniard beached upon these sands,
    Ready to lay his torch or violent hands
  On all he met : but that was long ago,
  And burn the mill was all that he might do
    Which named the place, but now no longer stands.

SONNETS OF THE LIZARD.

TO THE LIZARD.

I.

We drove betimes from Marazion town,
 Skirted Breage church, and, threading Helston
  streets,
 First sighted, where the tilth the moorland meets,
The Cornish heather roving on the down,
With full pale bells eyelashed with dainty brown.
 No heather such as this the sportsman greets
 As up and down his moor for grouse he beats
In Yorkshire or the Highlands. Cornwall's own
 It will not leave the sanguine serpentine
  And soil magnesian, but in this far place
 It blossoms and the marble gleams divine.
  'Tis like a dream some poet's pen might trace
 To have this strange fair stone and flower pressed
 In one wild corner of the scarce-known west.

II.

We lighted down and roamed across the moor,

   'Twixt stunted plants of heather and sea-pink,

   Until we found ourselves upon the brink

Of Kynance—Kynance with its sandy floor

And "Cow-rock" like a marble Kohinoor

   Blood - hued, upstanding.   When   the   sea   did
      shrink

   The " Bellows " brayed with every rise and sink

Of waves that round the island-base did roar,

   Even in the calm of a still summer day.

      In spacious caverns neath the cliff we walked

   With shimmering green and white and crimson gay

      For salon fit or banquet-hall, then stalked

   Along a dizzy path upon the isle,

   To gaze into the Devil's mouth a while.

III.

We left the isle and clomb the hill once more,
 Toward the Lizard, to the great twin lights
 Seen by the mariner on stormy nights
To warn him of the perils of the shore,
The "Lions' Den" where when the Lions roar
 No ship that sails could live,—so fiercely fights
 The lion breaker, from the rocky heights
Flung on succeeding lions. Thence we bore
 To where the terrace looks upon the cove
  Of fishy Cadgwith, picked our dubious way
To where we might gaze downward from above
  Into the "Devil's Frying-pan"; and day
Being far spent, our way then wended back
To Lizard-town to take the homeward track.

SONNETS OF ARTURIAN CORNWALL.

TINTAGEL.

AUGUST 1884.

TINTAGEL, huge rock-royal, glad was I
  That only here and there a crumbling wall,
  Hard to distinguish from the natural,
Still stood upon thy summit. Worthily
Could feudal palace-keep scarce occupy
  Such site ; and how would newer buildings pall
  Where every rood was stamped historical,
Or fancy-tinged, or steeped in legendry ?
  Dismantled, one can picture on the isle
    A shadowy Arthur washed up from the bay,
  And rear upon its front a stately pile
    Of marble as kings reared them in the day,
  Ere time had taught the Briton to neglect
  The lesson of the Roman Architect.

II.

Arthur and Ysolde, Uther and Ygraine,

    Tristram and Mark !—on moon-enchanted nights

    At murk mid-dark, or when the island's heights

Peer dimly through a veil of spray and rain

Driven by the western gales—ye live again.

    What wilder than this huge rock, ringed with bights

    Precipice-walled and reefy, for the fights

Of Uther and the Cornish Duke, both fain

    For Arthur's mother?   Not in fairy-land

       Have they in summer stillness such a cove

    With ferny caverns nooked and soft with sand

       To take a stranded babe.   And hate and love,

    Queen Ysolde's love for Tristram, and Mark's

       hate—

Thy smooth brow and dark chasms illustrate.

III.

I saw thee first late on a summer eve,

 Too dusky to distinguish the low block

 Of wall fast mingling with the native rock,

So dusky that I could not well perceive

The vast ravine the elements did leave,

 When the great drawbridge fell, before the shock

 Of giant storms or those strong dwarfs who mock

Adamant—mists which melt and frosts which cleave.

 Only the mount loomed black against the sky

  And at my feet slow heavy breakers roared,

 The while I trampled, musing wistfully,

  The stunted gorse and sea-pinks of the sward

 Upon the windy height, whereon still stands

 The church first founded there by Saxon hands.

IV.

Next morn I clomb the mount to seek the well
   And all but vanished earthworks. Those were
      there
When Uther's savage war-cry rent the air ;
Those and the mount itself alone could tell,
Had they but tongues, where such a hero fell,
   And such a gallant prince won such a fair,
   And how Queen Ysolde of the raven hair
Held the stout knight, Sir Tristram, in her spell.

   The month was August and the morn was grand
      With all that makes an August morning dear
   To rain-vexed England ; light the west wind chased
      The ripples on the bay ; the sky was clear,
   The sun shone bright, the air was warm and dry :
   And Nature held the keep of days gone by.

CAMELFORD—CAMELOT.

I.

Not Camelot the towered—the goodly town
  Upon the shining river, whither passed
  The Lady of Shalott, when fallen at last
A victim to her spell, slow-wafted down !
Not Camelot the towered, the glittering crown
  Of all King Arthur's cities !   Yet thou hast
  Thy legend of the King—how Modred massed
His traitor legions, where the waters brown
    Run neath the Bridge of Slaughter, how the King,
      With Launcelot dishonoured, Tristram slain
    And half of his Round-table following
      Dead or apostate—triumphed ; then was ta'en,
    Stricken to edath, by bold Sir Bedivere
    To Dozmary and passed upon the mere.

CAMELFORD—SLAUGHTER BRIDGE.

II.

In the soft prelude of an August night
  We sallied forth from Camelford in quest
  Of where his last great battle in the west
Brought death to Arthur.   Grey the gloaming light
Ere we were in the valley of the fight,
  A spot by Nature framed for fierce contest,
  With ridge commanding ridge, and crest on crest,
On either side a little river, bright
  With waving sedge and darting trout.   The bridge
    Was wreathed with blackhaired spleenwort and
        wild flowers,
  And the rank grass beneath the lowest ridge
    Guarded a stone, in characters not ours,
  Claimed by the country-folk with wondering eyes
  To tell that Arthur underneath it lies.

MISCELLANEOUS POEMS WRITTEN IN CORNWALL.

SIR HUMPHREY DAVY'S SEAT, GULVAL CARN.

Mousehole, Penzance, St Michael's at my feet,
 Severed by stretch of hill and rock and sand,
 But linked together with a gleaming band
Of glassy waves. This was Sir Humphrey's seat,
Which in bright youth he sought, for converse sweet,
 As youthful genius will in every land,
 With the shy Muse of Poesy, and scanned
The bay below and moors above replete
 With Beauty's grace and Freedom's.

       Few had thought,
 Unless they read the story of his youth,
That first his lamp the sage to Fancy brought
 And Wisdom afterward. But love of truth,
Like love of fame, imagination needs
To nerve it and inspire it to great deeds.

TO E. M. S.
AFTER A TOUR IN CORNWALL.

In solitary Zennor have we been,—

    Have trod Chun's mighty castle-heap of stones,

    And traced the barrows, where they laid men's bones

After some old-world battle waged between

The natives and invaders—gazed at Treen

    Rock-ramparted with boulder-bastions,

    As if a king of giants had lived there once

And forced his folk to build—we two have seen

    The Atlantic charge unbridled on the wall

      Of rock which shields the end of English land,

      Have had a calm blue sea on either hand

    At Galva's Carn, and watched the sunset fall

      And moonlight play and dawn its glitter fount

      Over the castle on the Guarded Mount.*

* St Michael's Mount.

MARGUERITES.

Lady in the Daisy's vesture,
　Dazzling white relieved with gold,
Free from all affected gesture
　As the flower, not too bold,
Though thou fearest nought, thou art
Truly the flower's counterpart.

For although in form and features
　There are few of womankind
Fair as thou, of all God's creatures
　Thou art humblest in thy mind;
Yet thou fearest not to stand
By the proudest in the land.

Just as, though in all creation
    Flower perfecter is not,
It is with its simple station,
    In a quiet garden-plot,
As content as though it were
In a palace sojourner.

Yet if on a queenly bosom
    In a chaplet it is laid
With the rose and lily-blossom,
    Though their worship first be paid,
Afterwards it is confessed
Lovely, if not loveliest.

Thou art upright as the flower,
    Art as purely raimented,
And thou hast a golden-dower,
    As it has, upon thy head,
And, like it, dost dread no stain
From the sun or wind or rain.

Farewell Daisies, flower-like maiden,

    And thou, flower-Marguerite !

May you be with dawn-dew laden

    Through the day to keep you sweet,

And no dust or heat of noon

Sully you or make you swoon !

BEHIND THE SCENES.

SOMETIMES it is man's privilege
To have a lovely woman, either sister,
Or, being wed himself, a friend
Who seeks his aid and counsel, if he list her,

And lays her mind before his eye,
Confesses herself simple and a mortal,
While those who are her worshippers
Regard her mouth as a Sybilline portal,

From which proceeds the voice of fate,
And look on her as a remorseless power,
That worship by caprice accepts
And tramples on her subjects in her hour.

While she, poor girl, is half appalled
By the immense importance thus accruing
To every little word or act
She has been saying carelessly or doing.

Her guide or brother sees it all,
How that she cannot venture to be simple,
However she desires to be,
When destiny is looked for in a dimple,

Doubt in delays and fate in frowns,
And love in happy peals of girlish laughter,
When aught she does or utters bears
She knows not what significance thereafter.

He, happy man, behind the scenes,
Seeing how hard she strives to do her duty
And so to act that what she does
May not deceive, must trebly see her beauty.

He knows, besides her outward charms,

That, far from being a remorseless power,

She is the fool of fate herself

And longing for the coming of the hour

When love will let her honestly

Her mind and heart implicitly surrender,

And let her give full liberty

To aspirations and emotions tender.

There is not aught more beautiful

Than watching a fair maid, who feels that beauty

Has won her love she would avoid,

But yet strives tenderly to do her duty.

THE CISTERCIANS.

"BEHOLD, bless ye the Lord, all ye servants of the
    Lord,"
Said the hoary-headed prior to the fair-haired chorister,
And rose the child's pure treble as his little heart
    out-poured
At matins and at even-song his praise in accents clear.

"Oh, ye that stand by night in the presence of the
    Lord,"
The hoary-headed prior's hand its task had finished
    now,
Was echoed to the chorister become a monk, who
    poured
His praise in dulcet tenor as he took the sacred vow.

O ye that in his courts do the service of our God,

" In the sanctuary lift your hands and bless his holy
    name,"

Sang the brother night and morning, as his holy path
    he trod,

Unceasing in his song of praise, and prior he became.

Bless ye, and may "the Lord that the earth and
    heaven made

Give you blessing out of Zion," in his accents shrill
    and thin

The chorister, long prior now and hoary-headed, said

To another sweet boy chorister but lately entered in.

To the fair Cistercian abbey by the stately river side

For many generations had the sweet-voiced boys
    been brought,

And first as choristers, then monks, had gently lived
    and died

In the perfect peace of God, since then elsewhere
    so vainly sought.

Their life was in their abbey locked, the stirring
world beyond
With its passions for fair women and its furious clash
of steel,
With its riot in high places and its curse and blow
and bond
For poor folk trampled down beneath oppression's
iron heel,

Was dead to them : 'twas not for hire or fame that all
day long
They wrought and laid the stones so well which made
their fabric rise
So glorious a temple for their morn and even-song,
With tower and spire and pinnacle all pointing to
the skies.

Their abbeys were not built ; they grew beneath the
brothers' hand
Till stones would bear no further touch they touched
no other block,
Like coral insects slow they worked, and like a coral
strand
Their work was perfect in its parts and solid as the
rock.

Twas not an age of architects who struggled to create
But one of building bees who worked harmonious for
 a whole
With one idea running through so obvious and great
That master's eyes were needed not to guide them to
 their goal.

The secret of the olden times which made the work
 they wrought
Like Nature's master-pieces stand the test of time and
 change,
Was that not fame or pay for work but perfect work
 they sought,
And knew perfection was a growth and not a product
 strange.—

Those frescoes with their humanness were Brother
 Clement's life ;
John to that missal's glowing page two scores of
 winters gave ;
That statue had for Brother Paul the graces of a
 wife ;
Two centuries of brothers wrought before they roofed
 the nave.

How shall we rear a work of art in our degenerate
    day,
A day when very plants are forced their products to
    forestall,
A day when seasonable growth is looked on as delay,
When architects scarce care for art and reckon labour
    all.

Just here and there an artist toils in the old-fashioned
    style,
Throwing his life into his task and throwing it in
    vain,
Only by merest chance his work will win the public
    smile,
And with it may be future fame through little present
    gain.

'Tis not that in these latter times the sum of art is
    less ;
We may not have the patient art to build a Gothic
    fane ;
But art is growing where was once a howling wilder-
    ness,
And even artizans can now its humbler flowers attain.

And poets make this overflow of art their joyous text,

Although they mourn the mighty men, the simple
antique folk,

Who laid each stone and limned each page, as if
there were no next,

And sowed their acorn quite content that it would be
an oak.

THE HARVEST.

I.

He scattered his seed in due season,
　But cruel the early frost ;
The rain and the sun were against him ;
　He dreamed that his crop was lost.

But later it waxed and it whitened,
　And harvesters gathered it in,
And some of it went to the windmill,
　And some of it bode in the bin.

And, after, they feasted and rested,
　The goodman along with his men,
For they knew that their work was over
　Till ploughing came round again.

II.

Was his brain-seed scattered in season
   Or early?   He long must doubt,
While censure with winter threatened,
   And after-neglect with drought.

But his brain-crop grew and it ripened,
   And the reapers, who seek good grain,
Had gathered the harvest exulting,
   And then he had sown again.

For little of feasting and resting
   Do the sowers of brain-seed know,
Till ploughing and sowing are over
   And they go whither all men go.

And when he is resting for ever
   His friends will they weep or rejoice,
Beholding the fruits of the sowing
   But missing the musical voice?

SYLVIA.

Sylvia are you, gentle Lady?
  Rightly Sylvia, recalling
Sunlight through the foliage shady,
  Cleft by morning breezes, falling.

Sylvia are you?   Woodland flowers
  Are as delicate as moon-light,
With no brightness and no powers
  Like the heather and the noon-light.

But the noon-light and the heather,
  Spite of all their strength and splendour,
Cannot match, the two together,
  With the Wind-flow'r's beauty tender.

"CORN AND ACORN,"

A PARABLE OF POETRY AND PELF.

Who soweth wheat, may see it whiten,
    When summer comes again,
And his and other homes may brighten
    Thus soon with goodly grain.

The ear has come, is ground, is finished,
    And he must sow again,
And work with labour undiminished
    To show one sack of grain.

But he who plants an acorn, planteth,
    What he may never see
A full-grown oak, but, if God granteth,
    Will one day be a tree

To shade not only those descended
From him who sowed the tree,
But fill with shape and verdure splendid
The gaze of all who see.

What wilt thou?—sow the grain, which whitens
In some few months and days,
To earn the ready pay which brightens
Life in so many ways?

Or sow the nut, which he who planteth
May never see an oak,
But which will grow, if God so granteth
A shelter to all folk,

A gladness to his kin and neighbours,
A glory to his land,
Proof when he long has done his labours
Of what his head and hand

Did for the spot where he was nourished
   Whole centuries before,
Though weaker men than he was flourished,
   While they were living, more?

What wilt thou?—sow with seed and gather
   The harvest of the day,
Or sow with nuts of promise rather
   Which may endure for aye?

THE LEGEND OF THE LILY AND THE ROSE.

SUGGESTED BY A PARAGRAPH OF THE LATE REV. R. S. HAWKER.

Do you know the old tradition
　Which would look on every Rose,
With its thorny crown as emblem
　Of the Christ who bore our woes,
Whatsoever be its colour,
　Whatsoever shape it grows?

And the Lilies of the valley,
　And the Lilies of the lake,
And the Lilies of the garden,
　Or whatever form they take,
As the emblems of the Mother
　Who bore travail for his sake?

You may talk of Tudor Roses,

    And of France's Fleur-de-lys,

Or the Lotus of old Egypt,

    But these flow'rs will ever be

Just the types of the sweet Saviour,

    And his Mother mild to me.

PART II.

ACROSS THE SEA.

MELBOURNE. January 1880.

On the S.S. "Lusitania."

I.

Past midnight had we watched the southern moon
 Illumining the long dark points of land
 Towards us stretched for miles on either hand,
And the broad bay still as a salt lagoon
On South Australian wilds; and now too soon
 The morn had come. Yet I leapt up and scanned
 With eager eyes the panorama grand,
When I was roused, a full eight hours ere noon,
 By the loud grating of the anchor chain;
 For Melbourne rose before me, silver-veiled
 From the dark wood of masts, which fringed the
 main,
 The port to which five thousand leagues I'd
 sailed,
 And greatest city of the southern sphere,
 Though she has not yet reached her fiftieth year.

II

I stood on deck still gazing eagerly,
  Till some one came and pointed out to me
  The landmarks, pier-lipped Sandridge by the sea,
The Scots' Church, the Cathedral-towers hard by,
The great dome looming out against the sky
  Where the world's exhibition was to be,
  And the blue hills of Dandenong, so free
And flowing in the distance. Presently,
  Ere seven bells had struck, a sailing boat
    Hove alongside and, sitting in the sheets,
  (Even now a hot wind blew), in thin silk coat
    I spied my host. How happy he who meets
His welcome at the threshold. Timely greeting
Is the best earnest of a welcome meeting.

III.

And my own Father's brother was my host,
  Though forty years had flitted since he went
  First forth from his ancestral home in Kent
To what was then the wild Australian coast.
And, though his home and kindred he had lost,
  Not vainly had his exiled years been spent,
  For in a corner of our Continent
A nation had been born, and he could boast
  That none of her distinguished sons had done
    More in the moulding of her destinies
  Than he, a steadfast man whom everyone
    Knew and respected—even enemies,—
  Leader of men in every fierce debate
  Though only few months leader of the State.

IN MEMORIAM.—SIR CHARLES SLADEN, K.C.M.G.

[BORN AT RIPPLE COURT, DOVER, 1816. PREMIER OF THE
COLONY OF VICTORIA IN THE CRISIS OF 1868. BURIED
IN THE CEMETERY OVERLOOKING THE SEA, AT GEELONG,
WHERE HE HAD RESIDED FOR FORTY YEARS, 1884.]

'Tis meet that he who dies away from home
  Should sleep beside the sea which links and parts
  His grave and ancient churchyards, where the hearts
Of those, who gave him birth, are laid in tomb.
'Tis meet, that when a strong man yields to doom
  His rest should be 'mid those for whom he fought,
  Amid the monuments of what he wrought,
And in some place to which all folk may come.
And therefore thou wert laid upon the hill
  O'erlooking the blue stillness of the bay
  Outside the city, where it was thy will
    In thy long sojourn forty years to stay,
  Far from the snowy cliffs which saw thy birth
  On the most famous island of the Earth.

II.

Thy birth was in the zone of pines, thy death
    Far from the cherry crofts and fields of corn
    And hop-clad hillsides 'mid which thou wast born ;
Far from the Severn stream that wandereth
(Past stately hall and bleak Salopian heath,
    With here and there a salmon in a pool)
    Where thou wert bred, at Philip Sidney's school,
Far from that other stream, that rivalleth
    The classic Isis in world-wide renown,
      Where thou didst make the study of the law
    And the bright page of history thine own,
      And from the great metropolis, which saw
    Thy happy wooing hours and studious days
    While thou wast conning Justice's dark ways.

GORDON'S TOMB.*

I MADE a pilgrimage to Gordon's tomb,
   And found him buried in a graveyard wild,
   By trivial sights and sounds all undefiled,
A sanctuary where field-flow'rs might bloom
Unapprehensive of their general doom
    Of being pulled by every wanton child,
    Or harrowed out and evermore exiled
For a crude, formal garden to make room.
   A broken column with a laurel wreath
     Marked where he lay; the murmurs of the sea
He loved in life forsook him not in death;
     The locust and the marsh-frog and the bee
Mingled their notes in one melodious breath,
     And near him blossomed a young wattle-tree.

* Written in the Cemetery at North Brighton, Victoria, over the tomb of Adam Lindsay Gordon, the poet of Victoria, born at Fayal in the Azores, and, like the author, educated at Cheltenham College.

II.

I cried out, surely this is as should be,

    The wild bard 'mid the wild flow'rs slumbering

    In a lone place, where wild birds go to sing,

In earshot of the everlasting sea.

Surely he would not sleep so easily

    (If there is after-life and ghosts can wing

    A flight to where their bones lie mouldering)

Had he been hemmed about with ceremony,

    With monuments of pride and gilt-railed beds

        Of far-fetched shrubs and plants.   Where now he lies

      The wild flow'rs of the new land rear their heads,

        And some we used in the old land to prize,

    The scarlet pimpernel with sleepy lids,

      And brier with bloom so delicate in dyes.

MELBOURNE.

JULY 1884.

QUEEN city of the South, electric spark
  Illuminating all our Continent,
   Thy motto is of conquest not content,
Thy rays are wide-spread through the primal dark
Of our mysterious north, thou stamp'st thy mark
  On territories of immense extent,
   And with potentialities up-pent
Within them as immense. Hark thou, O hark,
  The fairy bells are ringing to thy night
   Chimes of a day of wondrous brilliance :
  Begins to dawn thy future broad and bright
   Over the hills, and that which will enhance
Thy splendour, now is reddening the sky,
In token of a rich noon drawing nigh.

THE SOUTH-SEA VOYAGER.

[WRITTEN ON THE P. AND O. STEAMER " BALLAARAT," OUT
ON THE SOUTHERN OCEAN BETWEEN MIDNIGHT AND
DAWN.]

UNDER the starry southern sky,

Over the waters wide we fly,

The wavelets hiss around our bow,

Crested with foam deep-blue below,

To match the clear night overhead,

And the bright crescent moon hath spread

A belt of silver from our side

To where the sky and sea divide.

Over the spacious southern sea

A south-east breeze blows merrily ;

It fills the great black sails on high,

Standing out gaunt against the sky,

It lightly flecks the sea with foam

And speeds the good ship to her home,

With siren music round her bow

To lull to sleep the heads below.

Long after midnight I arise

And pace the deck with wondering eyes,

Revelling in the tropic air

Though slumber reigns supreme elsewhere,

Save on the Bridge where, looming black

Against the clear sky at her back,

The watch their lonely vigil keep

That others may in safety sleep ;

And in the throbbing engine room
Where ceaseless the huge pistons boom,
Driven by steam whose fires are fed
By swarthy blacks in Nubia bred ;
And forward, where a few Lascars
Crouch silently beneath the stars,
Waiting on their commander's lip
To do the working of the ship.

And first I raise my eyes on high
And gaze toward the southern sky,
To trace the starry-cross, then t'ward
The Hunter's gleaming belt and sword
I looked on in my native north
With child-eyes ere I wandered forth,
And lastly on the southern moon
So bright but doomed to waning soon.

The stars, the moon, the clear-dark sky
All lift the gazer's thoughts on high;
Surely the planets and the wind
Veil some omnipotence behind;
All surely would in chaos end
Did not some power their motions bend;
One cannot raise one's eyes at sea
And yet ignore the Deity.

Then I look downward, and the sea
Appals with its profundity,
One hundred times as deep as are
The highest masts on men-of-war,
And then its melody and hue—
So heavenly sweet so heavenly blue—
Its monsters and its marvels fill
My being with a mighty thrill.

Verily those who live on land
See not the wonders of God's hand,
But those who go down on the sea
In ships—who know the ocean's glee
When zephyrs blow, and know its wrath
When the South-Westers cross its path
And wind and water in their fray
Make mighty barks like aspens sway.

I sought my bunk again and dreamed
Of where the orange blossoms gleamed
Around my manhood's happy home,
Then flew in fancy o'er the foam,
To where the lime-trees in the spring
My childhood with soft green did ring,
Then mingled in confusion fair
The quick-set hedge and prickly pear.

Oh what a medley is my life—
With now a mother now a wife
For a Madonna—now the foam
Now terra firma for my home—
Now scorching sun, now cold and rain
To guard against—now groves of cane
And palm around me waving, now
Harebell and berry-laden bough !

But life—where'er—has charms for me,
Whether on land or on the sea,
In town or country, moor or wood,
In social throng or solitude,
Whether upon an Austral plain
Or in old Oxford once again,
In native London or Ceylon
The same fresh, happy, eager one.

THE TROPICS.

Love we the warmth and light of tropic lands,

   The strange bright fruit, the feathery fan-spread
      leaves,

   The glowing mornings and the mellow eves,

The strange shells scattered on the golden sands,

The curious handiwork of Eastern hands,

   The little carts ambled by humpbacked beeves,

   The narrow outrigged native boat which cleaves,

Unscathed, the surf outside the coral strands.

   Love we the blaze of colour, the rich red

      Of broad tiled-roof and turban, the bright green

   Of plantain-frond and paddy-field, nor dread

      The fierceness of the noon.   The sky serene,

The chill-less air, quaint sights, and tropic trees,

Seem like a dream fulfilled of lotus-ease.

II.

Strange is it that imaginative men
Should thirst so for the tropics? Kingsley passed
To Western Indies with a glad "at last,"
And seldom poet but has turned his pen
To paint their glories longingly : thrice fain
Was I, from childhood's earliest days, to cast
My lot where calm blue tropic waters glassed
The feathery palm and glossy-leaved plantain,
To watch the gay-clad natives with mild eyes
Carrying quaint wares or plying some quaint
trade,
To gaze where domed and gorgeous temples rise,
And lounge all day in the delicious shade
Eating rich tropic fruits, and witnessing
Some strangely fair or unfamiliar thing.

GUARDAFUI.

WRITTEN OFF GUARDAFUI.

A WEEK ago, we left the verdant shore

  Of Asia's pendent jewel, Taprobane,

  Palm-shaded to the margin of the main

And with rich fruits and foliage teeming o'er.

To-day we stand at Afric's Eastern door,

  Thee, Guardafui, home of the hurricane

  And heat and mist, whose grim slopes entertain

No single leaf. Thou seemest evermore

  Like a huge giant, watching the approach

    To Egypt's treasures, suddenly transformed

By Genies, whom thou lettedst not encroach

    Upon thy trust, into a stone, yet warmed,

With faithful rage, whenever ships intrude

Upon thy once scarce broken solitude.

ADEN.

WRITTEN OFF ADEN.

GIBRALTAR of the East, dark sentinel,
     Holding a shield over the waterway
     That floats ships to the cradle of the day
(Which was the cradle of the arts as well)
From the red west where shines the magic spell,
     Which once illumed the workshops of Cathay
     And India's temples with a magic ray
Of skill and science, we can scarce excel
     With all our boasted knowledge, thou art fair,
          Seen in the distance with thy lofty rock
          Twisted into grotesque similitude
Of mosque and castle in the evening air,
          Though thou art but a parched, pestiferous block
          Of barren stone, by nature unsubdued.

AT SUEZ. MAY 1884.

WRITTEN AT SUEZ.

IDLY the water ripples round the hull
 Of the great ship, detained in quarantine,
 And yet not wholly wasted will have been
Our day in Suez Harbour, beautiful,
Had it no memories time can not annul,
 The well that Moses found, the very scene
 Where Israel crossed the water-walled ravine
Formed by the rolled-back sea, and Pharaoh, full
 Of foregone victory, perished in the deep.
  So fairly do Arabia's hills and sand
 Mingle their rose and gold, where pilgrims creep
  From Cairo down to Mecca, on one hand,
 And on the other Egypt's in their hue
 Are dyed so gloriously dark and blue.

I

THE DESERT.

WRITTEN ON THE SUEZ CANAL.

SCORCHED rocks and sand stretching for leagues away,
  A few dwarf heaths, scant-leaved and choked with
    dust,
  Such was the land when Moses led his host
In flight from Egypt, such is it to-day ;
Although at noon may oft be seen a bay,
  Tree-fringed, which leads the traveller to trust
  That he has reached the palm-begirt sea-coast,
And that his parched and weary limbs shall play—
  When a few hours, a few more miles are o'er—
    In the clear waters mirrored silver-fair,
  Only to find an ever-stretching shore,
    Ever-receding sea. The mirage there,
  Is it not type of many a glittering hope
  That turned to rock and sand when we came up?

THE CANAL.

(SUEZ TO PORT SAID.)

WRITTEN ON THE SUEZ CANAL.

WE sailed along the narrow waterway
  Which links the dawn-tinged east and busy west,—
  A puny streak of water at its best,
E'en if it had not run through banks of clay.
Yet like the seal of genius it lay
  Upon the desert visibly impressed,
  E'en did not mighty steamers without rest
Press on, where all was land the other day,
  Like barges towing on an English river ;
    And when night overtook us on the lake
  Before Ismailia, we had not ever
    Viewed sunset fairer, so each crimson flake
  Was mirrored on the water, and the eve
  Round the strange town such radiance did weave.

FIANCEE.

WRITTEN ON THE MEDITERRANEAN.

ONLY a farce on shipboard it was true,
 And yet your genius is not oft excelled
 E'en by the Muse's daughters who have held
The stage in thrill, and so your beauty grew
Upon your audience, that they loved you too.
 Sweet were you, when you scornfully rebelled
 Against your ' Uncle's Will,' when you repelled
Your forced fiancé—doubly sweet when you
 Confessed your passion.   Soon the time must come
  For you to play the same part once again
 In life, to let dark eyes and wistful roam
  Over a manly face, held close, to rain
 Kisses like dew, to lay both tiny hands
 In a strong grasp and go where Love commands.

MALTA.

WRITTEN OFF MALTA.

I.

BLUFF island of so many memories
  Since the Apostle, shipwrecked on thy shore
  Gave thy rude folk a name for evermore
For kindness, and grew godlike in their eyes
By shaking off the snake, which did arise
  Out of the fire. I pictured o'er and o'er
  The ecstasy, with which I should explore
Thy knightly church, where the crusader lies,
  The halls where the grandmaster of St John
    Ruled like a prince, the walls of la Valette
(The jest and trophy of Napoleon)
    And mighty bastions the English set
Upon thy rocky brows—to see the work
  And waste of French and English, Knight and
    Turk.

II.

These and much more I thirsted to have seen,
　　And rose at earliest daybreak, full of hope,
　　Only to see the yellow flag run up
In token that we were in quarantine.
We caught some straitened glimpses of the scene
　　Even from the ship's deck, with its narrow scope
　　Narrowed yet more by deck-house, screen and rope.
We even rowed (to say that we had been
　　On Malta) to the Lazaretto.　So
　　　'Tis oft in life—some castle in the air,
　　Some city of the fancy, which did glow
　　　Through our existence, gloriously fair,
　　Is shut off by some tyrannous command
　　Forbidding us to foot the promised land.

CARTHAGE.

WRITTEN ABREAST OF CARTHAGE.

AT sunset we left Malta. Ere noon fell
 We passed Cape Bon, a lofty-crested cape
 Blue in the morn but indistinct in shape
Scarce known itself, but who hath not heard tell
Of Carthage? what high heart but loves it well?
 And Carthage lay behind the water-scape,
 Carthage still eloquent of Dido's rape,
Hannibal's vow and Hanno's citadel.

 My heart was stirred to think that where we sailed,
  Punic and Roman triremes oft had clashed,
 Until the youngest Scipio prevailed,
  And on one evil day to ruin crashed
 The glorious fabric reared by Tyrian hands
 With sea-borne spoil from all discovered lands.

GIBRALTAR.

WRITTEN OFF GIBRALTAR.

I ROSE at dawn and rising from the main
    Beheld the three peaks of the famous rock
    Which once withstood four years the surge and shock
By sea and land of banded France and Spain.
Grim were the heights from which the red hot rain
    Fell on the ships, igniting where it struck,
    And grim the mighty cannon trained to block
The entrance to the straits.   I looked again
    And saw the keep a thousand years ago
      Built by the Moor, with honourable scars
      Inflicted on it in long Spanish wars
    With Englishman and Arab. A proud glow
    Thrilled me, beholding where my countrymen
    So mightily endured, and not in vain.

TARIFA.

WRITTEN OFF TARIFA.

Two bells had struck when we Tarifa passed,
  Tarifa eloquent with memories
  Of Arab knights, and with its fortresses
Drenched with staunch English blood and now at
    last
On the Atlantic were we, heading fast
  For England.   Favourable was the breeze
  And blue the skies and mirrored blue the seas
And a spring sun a glittering halo cast
  Over the battered walls and ruined keep
  And quaint old Moorish houses, once the scene
    Of high Moresco pomp and chivalry,
  But widowed now and slumbering by the deep
  Beneath the sun of Africa serene,
    Unwakened save when the great ships forge by.

TRAFALGAR.

WRITTEN ON TRAFALGAR BAY.

CAPE TRAFALGAR ! O Bay of Trafalgar,
What Englishman can look unmoved on thee
While being borne on shipboard o'er the sea,
Where that October morn was seen afar,
Issuing in all the pride of naval war,
The banded might of France and Spain to be
Shattered in Nelson's crowning victory
Ere darkness fell.   O Cape and Bay ye are
Not grand or lovely, but ye illustrate
A truth as old as time, that humble things
Can be ennobled by endeavours great
Into a majesty unmatched by Kings.
Such is the halo heroism throws
Round every barren point on which it glows.

UPON THE S.S. "BALLAARAT."*

OFF USHANT.

DEDICATED TO THE HON. J. B. WATT OF SYDNEY.

O STATELY ship fast speeding to thy port,

    Our home, for six bright weeks of sunny weather,

    We have had many pleasant hours together

Since we embarked—voyagers of either sort,

Old Colonists returning to the land

    They left long since to win an independence,

    And young folks, born Australians, in attendance

Longing to see their Fathers' native strand.

We shall not leave our ship without a sigh,

    In which were born so many loves, hopes, fears,

    And friendships sure to last for many years,

Or the blithe officers, who brought us by

    Australia, Asia, Africa, to rest

    Safe in our dear old island of the west.

* A P. and O. Steamer.

AT PLYMOUTH.

At midnight we made out the Eddystone :
    An hour ere dawn, majestical and slow,
    We passed the iron fort, which daunts the foe
From Plymouth Sound, and dropped our anchor
        down.
At sunrise we took tender for Drake's town,
    And walked at early morn upon the Hoe,
    Where Drake his bowls would finish ere he'd go
To rock right to its base the Spaniard's throne
    And smite his ships.   We walked and looked once
        more
        Upon the long black ship which o'er the
        waves
Of Indian and Atlantic oceans bore
    Us safely home to look upon the graves
And mansions of our fathers, and to greet
Friends whom for years it was not ours to meet.

ICHABOD.

For forty years had aged Eli sate
Judging the tribes of Israel in the gate,
When God foretold to Samuel the doom
On Eli and his race about to come.
Early and late the man of God had prayed
And every precept of his Lord obeyed,
Except to lead his children in the path
By which they might escape their Maker's wrath :
And now the measure of his pilgrimage
Drew well nigh to an hundred years of age.
The aged man heard from the young child's lips
The doom which should his father's house eclipse,
And, as the quick tears of his woe outpoured,
He bowed his head and cried, " It is the Lord,
" Let him do whatso seemeth to him good,
And let His will by me be understood,
His be the will, mine the submissive mood."

To Shiloh on the even of the fight,
Whereon the Philistines did Israel smite,
With his clothes rent and earth upon his head,
There came a man of Benjamin, who said,
" Israel before the Philistines hath fled ;
Hophni and Phinehas thy sons are dead ;
The Ark of God is taken." With bowed head
The old man heard that both his sons were dead,
His people by the heathen undertrod ;
But when 'twas told him of the Ark of God,
Stricken with grief, he fell from where he sate,
And brake his neck beside the judgment gate.

Meanwhile the wife of Phinehas his son
Was great with child, her waiting wellnigh done,
And when she learned that Israel had fled
And that her Lord and her Lord's sire were dead,
And of the taking of the Ark of God,
She bowed and travailed, murmuring, "Ichabod,
The glory hath forsaken Israel,
The Ark of God is taken, and they fell,"
And when the womenfolk who looked thereon
Said, "Fear not thou, for thou hast borne a son
In place of sire and husband who are dead,"
She answered not nor heeded what they said,
But named the child her mournful 'Ichabod,'
Because the heathen had the Ark of God.

TWO YEARS OLD TO-DAY.

[Written upon the Second Birthday of the Author's Son at Struan, Toorak, Victoria, Nov. 25th, 1883.]

Two years old to-day !

And the sun ripples over the meadow

Rich with the breath of growing hay,

And there is not a sign of a shadow

On either flower-spangled scene

On the field with its azure germanders

And long grass stalks between,

Or the golden-haired infant who wanders,

Prattling his wonder merrily

Under the blue Australian sky.

Two years old to-day !

What of him in the march of the hours,

When twenty springtides trip away,

And the grass has been mown and the flowers

Faint with the early summer's heat,

And the banks upon which they were blowing

Are dust with trampling feet?

Golden-hair will have done with his sowing

And bare his sickle now to reap,—

God grant he may not have to weep.

Two years old to-day !

What of him in the march of the years,

When forty summers flow away,

And his mates have some reaped in their tears,

And some will have to reap no more,

And he owns to the scorch of the summers,

And has unbarred his door

To the little fair-headed new-comers,

And had himself to find the flowers

To brighten them in childish hours?

K

Two years old to-day !

What of him in his autumn and even,

When sixty years have slipped away,

And the shadows draw over his heaven,

And he looks back across his life,

Saying, " This day was good, and that glory

Was worth those years of strife,

And my name shall be written in story,

And as the founder of my race

My children's children I shall grace ?"

Two years old to day !

What of him at the fall of the night,

When eighty years have ebbed away,

And the golden hairs melted to white

Upon his last begotten son,

And his children of their lives are saying,

The done and the undone,

Since their golden-haired infancy's maying

Down in the flower-spangled glade,

Ere it was mown or in the shade ?

AN OLD ROMANCE.

A BAR of an old-fashioned waltz,
　　A glance at a faded dress,
What is it that wakes in my heart
　　These echoes of tenderness?

When that was the waltz of the hour,
　　That dress in its pride and glow
Of shimmering azure and pearl,
　　A seven of summers ago,

Sweet eyes used to gaze in my eyes,
　　Light fingers would clasp my own,
And a soft voice fell on my ears
　　In a tremulous undertone.

The face and the fingers I touch,

The voice in its music is here,

But Romance is a delicate moth

That lives—just the sweet of a year.

THE VALSE.

HE asks her a question; she answers yes,
With every grace in her graciousness,
And rises to yield him her slender form
Sweetly submissive and chastely warm,
Smiles as she rises and lifts soft eyes,
Gladdening when he would have her to rise,
Takes his hand firmly and leans on him,
Letting the rest of the room grow dim.

He only has asked for her hand to valse;

Her seeming submission and warmth is false;

Once after a valse, as she sat and fanned

The flush from her fairness, he asked her hand;

She rose with a motion of tender grace,

Yet did she not look him as now in the face,

But, drooping her lashes, besought him to go

Graciously—gracious even in no.

Her fingers in his have a touch of fire

To kindle the glow of the old desire;

The waist in his arm so submissive and slim

Awakes an electrical thrill in him;

He cannot encounter the tender eyes

Without piecing the broken reveries,

Or list to her voice in an undertone

Without dreaming of her as his yielded own.

Remembers she yet, when she yields to him,

So trustfully, fingers and body slim?

And does she remember, when, free from all wiles,

She offers him one of her own frank smiles?

Or feel, when she ushers her kind replies

With a pleading glance from her soft dark eyes,

How she kindles the flame of the sacrifice

Which is laid on her altar at such a price?

Fair maid, he would dance his whole life through,

Had he such a partner for life as you!

Fond man, she would dance not with you again,

Did she know that it brought back the old sweet
　　pain.

Yet cherish your secret and you may hold

Her waist in your arm, as you held it of old,

Press her hand, whisper—the vision is false,

It is not your love she accepts, but the valse.

THE GENTLEMAN-DROVER'S GOOD-BYE.

I.

Good bye, Old Chum !

We have, oft and on, been a lot together,

Under scorching sun, and in stormy weather ;

Even in the blaze we would often revel,

In the stormy days we defied the devil,

Took what might come.

II.

Good-bye a while !

When we two once more shall be found together

Goodness knows.   We are birds of one wild feather,

Here to-day and off once again to-morrow,

With just time to laugh or, instead of sorrow,

Grimly to smile.

III.

Until we meet,

Put on face as good for whatever weather,

As you know you would were we two together :

Don't believe I said single word against you :

Don't believe I did what may have incensed you :

Friend-trust is sweet.

IV.

Good-bye once more !

Friends like we two are soon must drift together

In the world somewhere, come what may in weather,

If we only make both our minds up to it,

You your oath may take we shall somehow do it,

No long time o'er.

THE QUEEN OF HEARTS.

SHE was the Queen of Hearts : there were some few
　　with beauties rarer :
This one had hair more golden-tinged ; that one had
　　bluer eyes ;
This was to the unheeding gaze unquestionably
　　fairer ;
That was more graceful, as she moved, or wittier in
　　replies.

But she was beautiful enough to dazzle in a measure,
With clear eyes blue enough to haunt a lover with
　　their hue,
With grace sufficient not to jar upon one's sense of
　　pleasure,
As she moved to you and light arch wit which on
　　the hearer grew.

Her crown was gentleness : her grace was graciousness
unfailing,

Soft smile or glance for everyone in all her court of
friends,

Her majesty a loftiness through her whole life pre-
vailing,

Which could not for a moment stoop to meaner
thoughts or ends.

THE SIGH OF THE SHOUTER.

GIVE me the wealth I have squandered in "shouting,"
    Scattered in sixpences, paid by the pound,
Ladled out glibly—no grudging or doubting,
    Never a thought of the use to be found?

Where are the hours that I wasted so gaily,
    Drinking and laughing in front of the bar —
Hours that I spent in mere indolence daily
    Heedless of how it my future might mar?

Gone, as the sun of the summer has vanished ;
    Woe with the winter is hurrying in,
Woe for the waste that can never be banished,
    Gone is the glitter, but stayeth the sin.

TO G. E. MORRISON, Esq.,

AN EXPLORER OF NEW GUINEA.

[A College Friend of the Author's at the Melbourne University.]

WHEN first I read romances as a boy,
 In playtime often used I to devour
 Stories of savage warfare by the hour,
And wild adventures filled my soul with joy.
As I grew older they began to cloy,
 Because I came to feel the sceptic's power,
 And look on tales of scalp and arrow-shower
As scarce less shadowy than the tale of Troy.
 But, when to Austral shores I winged my flight,
  Once more I stood upon enchanted ground,
  Adventure in its heyday still I found,
 One term at college missed a friend from sight,
 And heard that he his life had wellnigh lost,
 Exploring on the wild New Guinea coast.

II.

You should not be a disappointed man
   Although you did not light upon success :
   You had not failed, had you adventured less :
Wiser—as well as nobler—is the plan
To greatly dare, albeit you may scan
   Too high a goal, than yield in idleness
   To drudge on in the calling you profess,
Doing what men of smaller compass can
   Better maybe than you.   The while you deem
      That you were born to do His higher work,
      And to do petty labour were to shirk
   The task allotted to you in His scheme.
   For he who hath five talents doeth ill
   If he doth what one talent could fulfil.

III

We do not say that he has wholly failed,
Who much has dared though little has he wrought,
If, odds against, he gallantly has fought,
And over adverse circumstance prevailed.
For veterans 'twere something to have sailed
Into a savage land so thickly fraught
With pest and peril, as the shore you sought
And penetrated, (until spear-impaled
By lurking foemen), when you scarce could call
Yourself of man's estate.   More stir and strife
Have you imported into your brief life
Of two and twenty summers than befall
Most people in a life-time.   So much won
Advance upon the bright path you've begun.

AT WINDSOR, NEW SOUTH WALES,
IN WINTER.

THERE'S a reek from the stalks of the Indian corn,
    As they stand in their blazing sheaves,
There's a freshening breeze from the uplands borne,
    And a rustle of pelting leaves,
Which will bound in a moment across the lea,
    Like the flattest of pebbles thrown
For a duck and a drake on the summer sea
    By the children at Brighthelmstone.

Were it not for the smoke from the stalks of corn
    And the scent from the orange trees,
And the White-Gums, whose sober-hued tresses scorn
    The chill and the toss of the breeze;
Were it not for the Wattle with golden plume,
    And the She-oak with plaintive moan,
I could fancy that I was beside the tomb
    Of my mother at Brighthelmstone.

Yes! the trees, which are shedding, are English
    trees,
  But they grow not in English land,
And the wind has the breath of an English breeze,
  But it tastes not of Sussex sand,
And the heavens in winter had ne'er the hue,
  And a sun such as this ne'er shone,
And the scent on the orange bloom never blew
  In the gardens at Brighthelmstone.

It is, merry the glow of an Austral morn
  And the sun of its winter sky;
And the green of the burgeoning Indian corn
  Is a glory on earth to eye;
But as oft as I wander and weave my song
  On the balmiest day, alone,
For a moment I wish that I roamed along
  On the beaches of Brighthelmstone.

L

COOPER OF TUMUT,

A HERO.

[A TRUE STORY OF THE AUSTRALIAN BUSH.]

A HERO as gallant as he of Khartoum,

Though one met his rescue and one met his doom,

Was Cooper of Tumut, a six-year-old child,

Left lonely on guard in a New South Wales wild.

The township of Tumut stands sweet on the river,

In the serest of summers an oasis ever;

But our poor little hero lived deep in the hush

Surrounding the settler far back in the bush.

A little one ailing and tossing in bed—

Its father was working far off for its bread:

Its mother was nursing a babe at her breast,

With five little children to rob her of rest:

Her husband was working far off for their bread,
The little one ailing and tossing in bed :
With the babe at her breast and her six-year-old child,
In search of assistance, she plunged in the wild.

The track through the forest from clearing to clearing,
If trampled not often is aye disappearing ;
The gum-branches falling, the heaths that upspring,
So wanton is nature—a veil on it fling.

At eve in Australia the darkness is swift,
The shadows o'erwhelm like the snow in a drift,
And ere she had come to her neighbour's, the night
Had brought her to bay in the midst of her flight.

The night it was stormy ; the thunder-cloud showered
Its tears on the three, as for shelter they cowered
In a hole by the root of the tree that was nighest,
Defying the lightning which shivered the highest.

A day and a night with no morsel of food—
No breast for the babe—she must feed it with blood—
Her own, or the child's, or, the faithful to death—
The dog's, who would loather lose master than breath.

The dog must be slaughtered : he flies not away,
But welcomes the hand that is stretched out to slay :
This truest of Christians endures to the end
With the love that would lay down its life for a friend.

Oh ! many the morn that the children would rush
With the dog as sole escort to roam in the bush :
He'd bark for sheer gladness as outward they trooped,
And brought up the rearguard as homeward they
    drooped,

With his tongue hanging roguishly out of his mouth,
Perhaps in dog-laughter, perhaps for the drouth,
With a dignified march that declared without doubt
That he'd frisked off the spirits with which he'd set
    out.

He feared not to battle the deadly black snake,
That the little one wished in his fingers to take,
(When out in the forest with "Laddie" alone)
As it flashed in its sleep on a sunny flat stone.

What wanted the dingo found dead at the door,
With Laddie beside him half dead in his gore,
Which Father and Mother away for the night
Had found when they came to their children at light?

The friend of the children, the guard of the house,
Whom kindness could conquer, no teasing could
    rouse,
Must end up his life of devotion with death :—
If his blood might give baby an hour more of breath.

He died as he often had perilled to die,
For their lives that he loved—mild reproach in his
    eye,
That the hand which now wielded the gum-log that
    slew
Should be that he had licked with attachment so true.

The babe could not live upon loyal-heart's blood,
As it lived on the milk it was used to for food,
The slaughter availed not : the baby still died,
And the mother toiled on with the child at her side.

Three days and three nights and the baby was dead.
She bore her dead babe and her little one led,
And, fed with the flesh of the friend that had gone,
The little one still struggled manfully on.

Four days ! And the noontide glared down from the
    sky,
The merciless sun of Australia was high :
The stout little spirit could struggle no more,
And downward he sank on the forest's rough floor.

But stronger than Hagar the mother, who left
Boy and babe by the water still full in a cleft
From the rain of the thunder, till aid she had found
For the child on its bed and the child on the ground.

Two days more she wandered, unsheltered, unfed
Ere she came to the Chinese who gave her his bread,
And ran for a digger, miles further away,
To help him to succour the child left astray.

They hasted, but camped on the mountains that
    night,
For long ere they neared him they lost the day's light,
And when they did reach him, this six-year-old child
Had been three days alone without food in the wild,

Three days all alone without food in the wild,
This stout little hero, this six-year-old child,
In peril of serpents, in peril of dogs,
No roof and no pillow but sky and dead logs.

O singers of battles, no hero sing ye,
Who'd the soul of the Spartan more truly than he ;
This six-year-old child in Australia's bush
Would put half the soldiers of story to blush.

For there was the little one after his fast

Of a week in the bush, when no morsel had passed

His lips, save the dog's flesh before he was left

By his mother afaint near the pool in the cleft.

For there was the little one lying—ah no,

But sitting up, spite of his want and his woe,

By the little dead baby with vigilant eyes

To guard the poor body from hawks and the flies.

A hero as gallant as he of Khartoum,

Though one met his rescue and one met his doom,

Was Cooper of Tumut, this six-year-old child

Who stood as a sentry three days in the wild.

Envoy.

He eat and was rescued : mayhap in the years

He will live and will die in the simplest of spheres,

This child who has shewn in six years from his
     birth

A valour unpassed in the annals of Earth.

A BALLAD OF

WATTLE-BLOSSOM.

[THE NATIONAL FLOWER OF AUSTRALIA.]

WHEN winter is over and summer not come,
    When the North wind forgetteth to freeze or to sear,
When the tempests, which shout in September, are
        dumb,
    Nor the drouth, which we dread in December, is
        here ;
    When the children are out in the prime of the
        year
To gather a glory of tint and perfume,
    Though the Waratah, Rose, and Epacris are dear,
Yet it's hey for the Wattle with gold for its bloom.

When summer in splendour and swelter hath come,
 And the creeks are all dry and the grass is all
  sere ;
When the picknickers roam in the forest for gum,
 Which wells from the Wattle in carbuncles clear ;
 If little they gather when no one is near,
The sunny young girl, whose shy glances illume,
 And her sunburnt and stalwart and staunch cavalier.
Yet it's hey for the Wattle though gone has its bloom.

When the shy-glancing maiden has wandered from
  home
 To the land, where her forefathers hunted the deer,
Where the sky without cloud and the sea without
  foam
  Are a sight for the Gods, and Decembers are
   drear ;
  When she sighs for the sunburnt young squatter not
   here,
And picks from his letter, just brought to her
  room,
  The blossom he plucked in the prime of the
   year,
Then it's hey for the Wattle with gold for its bloom.

ENVOY.

When children are out in the prime of the year
　To gather a glory of tint and perfume—
When shy-glancing maiden meets staunch cavalier,
　Then it's hey for the Wattle with gold for its
　　bloom.

LIGHT AND SHADE.

[WRITTEN AT OLD GOVERNMENT HOUSE, PARRAMATTA,
NEW SOUTH WALES.]

BENEATH an Austral winter sun,
   A worn man and a little child
Roam in a garden, overrun
   With creepers and with beds gone wild;
The one with sallow sunken cheek
   And doubled back and wasted hands
And hollow voice and motions weak
   Telling of years in tropic lands,
The other revelling in wealth
Of careless joy and glowing health.

They both are idle : one doth pause
    Since now his day for work is done,
The little laughing child because
    His day for work hath not begun :
They play together—the worn man
    Finding the infant's tricks and talk
Able to exorcise and ban
    The doubts that dog his daily walk,
The wondering infant glad to find
One so unoccupied and kind.

The worn man sought the gentle clime
    Of this delightful, genial land,
Feeling that else in no long time
    He would be gathered to God's hand.
The little sunny child was born
    In this same sunny continent,
As full of morning as this morn,
    In which the warmth and cool are blent
In that proportion just, which gives
Health and delight to all that lives.

THEMISTOCLES

TO THE PEACE PARTY AT ATHENS,
BEFORE SALAMIS.

SIRS, you've lived somewhat longer than we have,
And are so much the nearer to the grave,
And, if you can win these few years of peace,
Think that your pilgrimage on earth may cease
In your old selfish indolence and ease
Beside your vines and olives and fig trees.
But we are young and are not fain to live
Upon such welcome, as the Hellenes give
To those, who have no portion or estate,
But within strangers' walls do congregate.

WORDSWORTH'S "TWO VOICES."

[WRITTEN AT WAVERLEY, GEELONG, VICTORIA.]

"Two voices are there : one is of the sea
   One of the mountains : " so the Poet sung,
   Who lived the hills of Cumberland among,
And gave their names, O Liberty, to thee,
But they have a significance for me
   Sweeter than liberty, less steeped in wrong,—
   Home—for I too in days when I was young,
Lived on those Cumbrian hills.
                 And, though there be
Five thousand leagues of sea between us set,
   Oft as the peaks of distant hills I've scanned,
I've dreamed of Easdale's mountain-coronet,
   And when upon the ocean's brink I stand,
I see in it a chain of blue and foam,
To link me, long drawn out, with my old home.

POETS.

[DEDICATED TO GEORGE P. E. SCOTT, ESQ.]

HE is a poet, who lays stone to stone,
 As well as he who builds the lofty rhyme :
 We have stone poems dating from the prime
Of Athens, and three thousand years have flown
Without the ivy of oblivion
 Loosing one fragment from the pile sublime
 Reared on Troy's ashes in the elder time
By the blind islander. The Parthenon
 And Iliad are ideas alike in kind
  But told in divers forms. It matters nought
What the material moulded to the mind,
  If the result matches the artist's thought.
One builds a stately pleasure-house in rhyme,
And one a poem writes in stone and lime.

THREE GRACES.

[C——, I——, and E——.]

ONE hath sun-brown, one gold, one auburn hair ;
   Each hath blue eyes, and each the damask cheek
   Of pink and white, the profile of the Greek,
The graceful form, the foot that treadeth air,
The worship of the beautiful and rare,
   Swift intellect, simplicity antique,
   Courage against the strong, and for the weak
Soft pity : each is feat and frank and fair.

One hath the spell of music in her fingers,
   And one the art of Raphael, the third
That witchery of voice which oft-times lingers
   In memory years after it is heard ;
And all—to a fair edifice fair dome—
Are useful, homely women in their home.

M

B. A.

Free,

To go for a scud on the sunny sea !

The study at morning and midnight done,

The scribbled old books on the sofa thrown,

The ink-pot left open to choke with dust,

With an old J nib in it stiff with rust,

And a red and blue pencil, in need of cutting,

Sticking out of a drawer too full for shutting.

Done !

And now I am free for a bask in the sun,

Or reading a legend of ancient birth

Of men, who have long since mingled with earth

On the shores of the Mediterranean,

Or to watch how Irene toys with her fan

To eke out a story, as old as Adam,

When Monsieur Moustache is with beautiful madam.

All !

Are you sure that my " scout " will not give me a call,

To be up with the lark and retrieve the work

That overnight pleasure had made me shirk ?

May I chat over lunch and have out my sleep,

Without having one eye on the clock to keep?

May I once again act as if I was human,

And venture to look on the charms of woman ?

Yes !

That vision has passed in its hideousness :

Henceforth, without favour or fear, I can

Look the world in the face, and stand up a man :

For no tyranny crushes the heart and soul

With its cruel exactions of time and toll,

Like that which determines so much our station

In life—our arch-bogy—examination.

THE BARBED ARROW.

THEY tell me he is light of love,
  And cares for no one well,
That wont his fancy is to rove
  Like fawns upon the fell.
I know not this, I know not aught
  Save that we are apart,
And oh ! I would that I had caught
  The key-note of his heart.

'Tis not that we have plighted troth ;
  We never spoke of love,
But just the glad converse of youth
  With laughter interwove.
'Twas thus, they say, he used to talk
  With many another maid,
Amid the glory of a walk
  By morning in the glade.

Alas it is not morning now,
　　And he is not with me ;
And yet I am his own I vow
　　Whosever own he be ;
If he has loved so many well,
　　Loved by so many been,
Does it not prove him loveable
　　Although it prove my teen ?

O voice of youth and mirth come back,
　　And wear his own dear form,
To haunt the old familiar track,
　　With friendship's rays once warm,
Though other maids were there before
　　And others on me press,
O suffer me to make one more
　　And spare me one caress !

PART III

POEMS
WRITTEN IN LONDON.

THE EXILE'S RETURN.

ONCE more he stood in the home of his childhood;
  Once more he walked 'mid the chestnuts and limes;
The trees were as green in the glory of springtide;
  The house was the same, yet 'twas not like old
    times;
  For he was but a guest where he had been a son,
  And the home of his childhood for ever had gone.

His parents were there, and more tender than ever;
  But the brothers and sisters, with whom he had
    played,
Had been fledged and had taken their mates and had
    flitted,
  And the one who behind in the nest had still stayed
  Was the child of his parents' old age, just the one
  Who had not with him from his childhood upgrown.

And he learned the sad truth that when once the
    fledged nestling
  Has forsaken its place in the nest, it grows cold,
Though the parents be warm, and however he presses
    It never will have the same glow as of old,
    And the bird who has once made a nest of his own
    Can never go back to the nest he has known.

O nestling forsake not the nest of your parents !
    O nestling be slow to be fledged and to fly !
'Tis so easy for brothers and sisters to scatter,
    For parents and children to sever their tie ;
    And the nestful, once broken, can never be one
    In the way which it was ere the breaking was done.

The limes, while they live, will be green in the spring-
    tide ;
  The chestnuts will blossom in April and May ;
But children, who once leave their homes, will return
    not,
    Or, if they return, it will not be to play
    And to nestle together ; it is not their own,
    But the home of their parents when once they have
    flown.

THE POET.

The Poet, writing, feels nor heat nor cold
Nor thirst nor hunger as he doth unfold,
While his rich mind is open, from its hoard
The gorgeous pageantry, with which it's stored.
Winter or summer outside matters not ;
'Mid winter snows he can enjoy a hot
And peerless day in palm groves of Ceylon,
And, 'mid the scorching desert, can dwell on
The breezy Kentish Cliffs, where he was born,
In all the glory of an April morn.
And, though not rich enough to keep a wife,
Omnipresent in day-dreams of his life
He can have some pure image heavenly bright,
Some woman, of a dazzling grace and light
Denied to kings, almost as much imbued
With life as if she were real flesh and blood.

He wants no worldly store of costly things,

For he can have for the imaginings,

In turn, the fancifulness of Japan,

The glow of Ind, old art Italian

Or English luxury.   His home can be

By some wild fiord of the northern sea,

Or in the peerless lands neath southern skies

Peopled by English blood and enterprise.

His house can be some ancient Gothic keep

Or wide verandahed bungalow, where sleep

Reigns through the fiery middle of the day.

Alone, his converse can be grave or gay ;

And he is in best company alone,

With none to interrupt the magic tone

Belled from within, a kind of mystic chime

Rung by the fancy to the ear of time.

Give him enough to clothe himself and feed

Without his care, and he is rich indeed,

Able to revel when they both so choose,

In undisturbed communion with his Muse.

Dependence is his foul fiend, and restraint,
To have to listen to one drear complaint,
To finish long and uncongenial tasks,
To leave his Muse, when some small tyrant asks.
Freedom is aye the burden of his song,
For he is left one of the common throng
If from constraint and care he is not free
To give himself up to his phantasy.

But it is hard for woman, who is real,
To wed one ever wooing the ideal,
To have the few brief minutes when, tired out,
He cannot follow the will-o'-the-wisp about,
To have him in his uncongenial moods,
When he is unfit for his solitudes,
To live on crumbs of comfort, which may fall
From the rich table, where he feasts with all
The grand guests of his fancy—go through life
More as his children's mother than his wife.

For if a woman is a poet's ideal
His Muse is ever worsted by the real,

And all the poetry, which would have gone
Into his written poems, is lavished on
His poem-life, known only to himself
And his soul's Queen; and when laid on the shelf
After his passionate life-time, lost for aye,
Unless some friend who knew him in his day,
Falls back on that life-poem for the plot
Of a romance, writing what he wrote not
But lived.   We cannot in this world have both
To indulge in the bright intercourse of youth
And also haunt the shady cloisters where
There lurks an inspiration in the air.
The Muse's husband cannot have a wife,
Like other men, the essence of his life.

"MAMMON AND POESY;" OR,

"THE POET'S CHOICE."

[DEDICATED TO ROBERT BROWNING, ESQ., D.C.L.]

"The elder Mr Browning had but two children—
the poet, and a daughter, who still keeps house for
her brother. When the son had arrived at that age,
at which the bias or opportunity of parents usually
dictates a profession to a youth, Mr Browning asked
his son what he intended to be. It was known to
the latter that his sister was provided for, and that
there would always be enough to keep him also, and
he had the singular courage to decline to be rich.
He appealed to his Father whether it would not be
better for him to see life in its best sense and culti-
vate the powers of his mind, than to shackle himself
in the very outset of his career by a laborious training
foreign to that aim. The wisdom or unwisdom of
such a step is proved by the measure of its success.
In the case of Mr Browning the determination has
never been regretted, and so great was the confidence

of the Father in the genius of the son, that the former at once acquiesced in the proposal."—*From* "*The Century Magazine,*" *Dec.* 1881.

WEALTH came to him with outstretched hand,
  And said, " Young dreamer come with me
And have the fatness of the land
  And costliest gifts from o'er the sea."

He took him to the mountain-top
  Of Mammon, shewed him all the Earth,
The good things for which all men hope,
  Which the world holds of highest worth,

And said, " Bow down and worship me,
  And all thou seest shall be thine ;
The glories of the land and sea
  And fulness of the Earth are mine.

" But know I am a jealous God,
  And he, who worships me, must tread
All day in crowded alleys trod
  By hard coarse men—must leave his bed

" Early and seek his pleasure late,

 An altar of his desk must make

And missal of his ledger, wait

 Until his sacrifice I take.

" Then he can trample on the lives

 And souls of those who cross his path,

Can choose himself a wife of wives,

 Can make lands tremble at his wrath,

" Can eat and drink whate'er is best

 In either sphere, can clothe his limbs

With whatsoe'er is costliest,

 Live in a palace, list to hymns

" Extolling every little crumb

 From his rich table let to fall —

Until his day of death may come,

 A kind of monarch over all."

N

He finished but, the while he spoke
 In tempting accents to the youth,
Over the distant hills there broke—
 Over the distant hills of truth—

A gleam of sunshine glowing on
 A far-off vision. She was fair
The maid on whom the sunshaft shone
 And with a crown of glittering hair,

Which changed in colour, as the sight
 Of him who saw was toned to view,
Now golden-bright, now dusk as night,
 Now dull and now of sunny hue.

But there was this about the maid
 That he, who at her beauty's shrine
Had worship once or homage paid,
 Could ne'er his fealty resign,

But through howe'er a chequered life,
    Come good, come ill, in wealth or want.
Though great in state, though with a wife
    Fair as a queen, must ever haunt

Her altar with a sacrifice
    Of longing, whether of regret
Or hope, and with some quaint device,
    Such as the old Knight-lovers set

Upon their casques when they essayed
    Their prowess 'neath their lady's eyes—
Even in the distance was this maid
    Wondrously fair to his surmise.

She drew no nearer than to speak
    In tones just loud enough to hear,
And yet 'twas not in accents weak
    But rather in a whisper clear,

And thus she spake, " Come thou with me,
I have no Kingdom on the Earth,
And yet is not by land and sea
What men esteem of equal worth

" As my true speech, which many hear
But cannot write it down, and he
Who writes it is proclaimed a seer,
The one man of his century.

" I have no kingdom : thou may'st roam
Through all the oases of the world,
From where the millions make their home
To where no flag was e'er unfurled,

" From cosy cot by love illumed
In some new city's panting heart,
To old-world palaces exhumed
From neath Vesuvius' lava swart,

" Now over an Australian plain
 Of peaceful victories with sheep,
Now countries glorious with stain
 Of battle and with shattered keep,

" And whether 'mid the pines thou sweepest
 Of the free, valiant North, or 'mid
The glowing luscious East thou sleepest
 Until the day in dusk is hid,

" And whether in a Lady's bower,
 Or waging warfare thou shalt be,
Whate'er the place, whate'er the hour,
 Come good, come ill, on land or sea.

" The restless spark within thy torch
 Shall die not, howso low it gleams :
Thou wilt not need a temple porch
 To worship me as it beseems.

·"Once more, if thou my words canst hear,
  And write down truly what thou hearest,
Folks will bow down to thee as seer,
  Of all men to the gods the nearest.

" I cannot give thee life or wealth,
  Or rest, the crowning gift of Earth,
But if Heaven gives thee life and health,
  And thou art seer,—there's nought of worth

" But men will haste to offer thee
  As singer and interpreter
Of the lost voices, which there be
  Lurking within the earth and air."

The youth paused not,—though Mammon gave
  His gifts for certain undelayed,—
For a few years to be a slave,
  Then lord of all that he surveyed,

Though Mammon took him by the hand,
   And Poesy stood on the height,
And promised nought but only planned
   His guerdon if he heard aright,—

But took the torch which she did proffer,
   Content upon her altar stairs
One more bright, blasted life to offer,
   If Heaven heeded not his prayers

That he might be elect to write
   In language whoso ran could read
Voices from old towns borne at night
   And on still mornings from the mead,

Voices of Nature, Poesy,
   Or inspiration—what you will—
Heard when afar from human eye,
   Heard best when human sounds are still.

And Heaven listened : now he stands
A singer and acknowledged seer
Loved in all English-speaking lands,
In his own walk without a peer.

PART IV.

POEMS
WRITTEN IN DEVONSHIRE
CHIEFLY AT TORQUAY.

A BALLAD OF PLEASURE.

WE workers, who toil in the grimy town,
    Have heard of the drones who will spend the day
In galloping over the breezy down,
    Or sailing about on the bright blue bay,
    Or striving the strenuous hours away
In matches at cricket and games at fives,
    Or hunting or shooting or - - - - all in play,
While we are in slavery all our lives.

We workers, who toil in the grimy town,
    Have heard of the drones who will spend the day
In changes and changes of suit and gown,
    And vying each other in vain display,
    And lounging and lunching and idle say,—
Old bachelors wooing to wild young wives,
    Young bachelors losing their lands at play—
While we are in slavery all our lives.

We workers, who toil in the grimy town,

    Have heard of the drones who will spend the day

In dreaming away by the waters brown

    When summer is singing his roundelay,

    And over the fire, when in widow-grey

The winter once more from the north arrives,

    Just prating of Letters and Art in play,

While we are in slavery all our lives.

ENVOY.

We wonder what profit is theirs and say,

    " These indolent drones with their wasteful wives,

They shall not endure in their endless play,

    While we are in slavery all our lives."

A BALLAD OF PAIN.

The " Ballad of Pleasure " was finished at 1 a.m. on Feb. 1st 1885 : at 9 a.m. " Bob " was found dead in his Cradle.

My heart was overfull with joy,
　　As late I sat one winternight,
Exulting that my two-months' boy
　　Should now receive the chrystom rite ;
　　But, when the morrow morn was light,
My heart was overfull with pain,
　　For there I found him stiff and white,
The babe who never moved again.

My heart was overfull with joy,
 As late I sat one winternight,
Exulting o'er a two-days' toy,
 A ballad ready now to write;
But, ere the sun had climbed his height,
 My song was in another strain,
For there I found him stiff and white,
 The babe who never moved again.

My heart was overfull with joy,
 As late I sat one winternight,
Two hours of gold without alloy
 To pass with maidens boon and bright;
At morn I saw another sight
 Than maidens fair and maidens fain,
For there I found him stiff and white,
 The babe who never moved again.

ENVOY.

Many a sight of joy and light
May I forget, but not the pain
With which I found him stiff and white,
The babe who never moved again.

A BALLAD OF A GRAVEYARD.

[To WILLIAM NIMMO, ESQ., A COLLEGE-FRIEND
OF THE AUTHOR.]

THE Graveyard looks on Mary's Church ;
　And Mary's Church looks on the sea ;
And there I found with loving search,
　Not far off from a cypress-tree,
　A bed for his mortality,
Within the echo of the main,
　Our gleaming link that is to be,
When we are overseas again.

The Graveyard looks on Mary's Church;

  And Mary's Church looks on the sea;

The rain the chapel panes did smirch

  While I knelt down in agony,—

  I, and one college friend with me,

Oft mate in pleasure, now in pain,

  And comrade oft, I trust, to be

When we are overseas again.

The Graveyard looks on Mary's Church;

  And Mary's Church looks on the sea;

And there we sowed 'mid pine and birch

  A seed of immortality.

  And I, where'er on earth I be,

Shall never hear the sounding main

  Without this solemn memory,

When we are overseas again.

O

ENVOY.

We sowed his small mortality
   To sight the church which sights the main,
Our link with him that is to be
   When we are overseas again.

MAIDENHOOD—A SERENADE.

My Lady she loves me, she loves to be near,
She tells me—and oft—that my friendship is dear;
But, if I dare whisper one hint of my love,
Turns cold as the Lady of Even above.

Her heart is as warm as the Lord of the Day,
Her sunshine is clouded when I am away,
And yet if I venture that question to ask
Which, granted, allows her for ever to bask,

She flies to the shadow, which bashfulness throws
To check the sun's fervour from forcing the rose;
And days of coy wooing but slowly recall
The sunshine of friendship when shadows befall.

Were women as sunny, in wooing as we,

The shadows which chequer our courtship would flee ;

Were men but as mooncold in wooing, their lives

Would seldom be lit with the sunshine of wives.

She loves me, my lady :—she stays in the sun,

Though doubting, for aid, to the shadows to run ;

The rosebud is blushing to ope to the heat,

And the scent, as she bursts into blossom, is sweet.

My lady, she loves me, and whispers it oft,

Not timid and cold now but timid and soft ;

Both morning and even her sun she'd have light,

Like the sun of the north upon midsummer night.

UNDER THE MISTLETOE.

Why did he kiss her not? because he loved her;
    Because an angry word, a struggle vain,
    Might breed a coldness which should long remain:
The blushing maid but strove, as it behoved her.

Would it have pleased him, had she yielded lightly
    To every lip, which sought her cheek to taste,
    Under the mistletoe by frolic placed
Over the door, while laughter echoed brightly?

Why no! she had his worship : it would waken
    A rude surprise to see his Artemis,
From the high-places where he shrined her, taken,
    As if she were no coyer than Cypris,
And the pure dew from off her sweet mouth shaken,
    The virgin dew, by mirth and mischief's kiss.

II.

Why did she let him not? because she loved him,.
  Because if he, why not some others too,
  Because she'd have him think her chaste and true :
Why did he try? because it so behoved him.

For had he not long worship to her offered,
  Smiled with her smiles, grieved with her griefs, and
    talked
  Sweet music of the heart, as oft they walked,
And love in every speech but tongue-speech proffered?

Would she have let him with none by to see her ?
  Yes ! had he dared defy her first fierce speech,
Pinion her struggles, flat-refuse to free her,
  Kiss off her shame and anger, then beseech
Her love in spoken words, he might decree her
  Submissive lips and hands to him to reach.

III.

Under the mistletoe, who holds her hands now
  Out-stretched submissively, and yields her lips,
  Without demur, to love's repeated sips,
Delighting in her newly-fitted bands now ?

Is this the girl-Lucretia, who repelled him,
  With crimson-mantling cheek and shrinking form,
  And with reproach half-pleading and half-warm,
So that half-fear, half-penitence withheld him ?

If she had suffered him in jest, she could not
  Have yielded him so full a gift in fee ;
If he had plundered her in jest, he would not
  Have found his feast so rich when he was free,
And though his will in wrath she had withstood not,
  Without the grace of self restrained would be.

KING CHARLIE.

[Written upon the Third Birthday of the Author's
Son.]

Charles the Bold and Charles the Bad,
　　Charles the Great and the Victorious,
Set beside this little lad,
　　Where are now your triumphs glorious—
If the living dog is held
　　Better than the slaughtered Lion,
As the prophet wrote of eld?
　　Ye are shadows like Ixion.

Charles the Martyr, Charles the Mad,
  Charles the Swede and Charles the Hammer,
Ye, for all the pow'r ye had
  Not one syllable can stammer.
Yonder boy, in slumber calm
  Dreaming of some fairy story,
Has more strength in his right arm
  Than have ye for all your glory.

With the fair white robes of youth,
  Childhood's golden crown upon him,
Only the bright side of truth
  Told him yet, do we enthrone him.
Use thy power well, small king!
  Thou hast all the world before thee :
If thou lose it dallying,
  We can never quite restore thee.

Are their names remembered still,
  Having gone not as their cares have?
Yes, for few do deeds that will
  Stand the test of time as theirs have.
Yet these Charleses, in their day,
  Though the world could scarce contain them,
Now that they have passed away,
  Little board-school boys arraign them.

Child King Charlie, anxious eyes
  On thy future are directed:
Is the monarch we so prize
  Worthily a king elected?
Who shall tell us,—if there be
  No such thing as after-life time,
If no resting-place have we
  After labour-time and strife-time?

Charles the Swede and Charles Martel,

   Charles the Great and the Victorious,

History hath loved you well ;

   May this small king be as glorious !

May your good alone proceed,

   And this child illuminate,

Charles Martel and Charles the Swede,

   The Victorious and the Great !

TO A LADY ON HER TWENTY-SECOND BIRTHDAY.

E. M. N.

I KNEW you when, scarce more than child,
  You had but now left school,
A little shy, a little wild,
  A madcap of misrule.

I treasure yet the greeting smile,
  The dainty change of hue,
That fluttered through your cheeks awhile
  At our first interview.

Welcome and graciousness were writ
  As now upon your face,
Although you had not all your wit
  Or all your present grace.

By you I lived two golden years
   Beneath a cloudless sky,
Without a thought of wrath or tears,
   In closest sympathy.

I watched the growth of that sweet flower
   We call your womanhood,
Saw it develop hour by hour,
   Each leaf and blossom good.

Daily the blossoms sweeter grew,
   More shapely in their growth,
While kept the leaves the tender hue
   And softness of their youth.

You were like sister, in a land
   Where sisters I had none,
To whom I told whate'er I planned,
   And shewed whate'er I'd done.

While neighbours never spoke we word
We fain had spoken not,
And nought between us e'er occurred
Which we should wish forgot.

And then we left the dear old place,
I in fresh lands to roam,
And you with travel to efface
The loss of your old home.

Once more a few brief weeks we spent
In the familiar town,
But not in the old way which lent
To every hour its crown.

For cares we could not obviate
Kept us too far apart,
Although they varied not the state
Of friendly heart to heart.

We parted once again to roam,
    Whither we scarce had planned,
Until we found—myself at home,
    You in my native land.

We met, not as we parted last,
    But as we first had met,
As if two absent years had passed
    Just for us to forget.

We met with no distracting care
    To pilfer precious hours,
And reinstalled the friendship rare
    Which in old days was ours.

And then I saw the stately growth
    Of your full womanhood,
Still with the tenderness of youth,
    As with spring leaves, endued,

And with rich blossoms of the mind,
And blossoms of the soul,
In hue and scent and shape refined,
Harmonious with the whole.

Ungracious words you never spoke,
Or did once graceless act,
Nor pet illusion ever broke
For want of woman's tact.

Fair women were my idols e'er;
Sweet maids have I known well,
But never one, where soul more fair,
In fairer shape did dwell.

White soul the Roman bard would call
The spirit in your breast,
And this expression—all in all
Portrays its pureness best.

As years roll on, we two shall roam

O'er many a sea and land,

But I shall always feel it home

Where I can hold your hand.

A TALE OF TWO COLLEGES.

[An Echo from Cheltenham.]

She'd big, brave eyes of tender blue,
 The maiden at " The Ladies' College,"
And wavy hair of some soft hue,
 The maiden at " The Ladies' College,"
A mouth for love and laughter meet,
A voice for song and soothing sweet,
Her very trip was exquisite,
 The maiden at " The Ladies' College."

This maiden oft I chanced to see,
 In days when I was at " The College,"
And yet I swear was nought to me,
 In days when I was at " The College."
Eyes were but eyes, however blue,
Hair simple hair, whate'er the hue,
If she were fair I hardly knew
 In days when I was at " The College."

I wooed a coy "Eleven Cap," *

    In days when I was at " The College,"

Won my " twin C's " † mid hack and rap,

    In days when I was at " The College."

I dreamed of class-room victories,

Of " coming through the scrimmages,"

Of " driving fours " and " cutting threes,"

    In days when I was at " The College."

Nous avons changé. . . years ago—

    It may be ten—I left " The College,"

And other dreams more brightly glow

    Than boy-dreams, born when at " The College."

I care as much for " cutting threes,"

I like to look at " scrimmages,"

But I would give the world to please

    That maiden at " The Ladies' College."

---

* The badge of the Cheltenham College Cricket Eleven.

† The badge of the Cheltenham College Football Fifteen.

SYMPATHY.

DENY you that your body ails?
Oh then it is your mind that pales :
If Sickness darkens not your eye,
Her foster-sister, Grief, is by.

A gentle woman not a weak,
No trifle blenches your brave cheek ;
A Spartan of the Christian strain,
Despise you only your own pain.

I cannot share your pain or woe,
Until its source you'd have me know ;
Nor may I, what I feel, express
Till lips as well as looks confess.

But you have read my sympathies
In the mute message of my eyes,
Although you knew not that your pains
Awoke in me the kindred strains.

SEASONS.

His Spring! The hedge, which ran beside
  His father's cottage-door, was gay—
He was a village boy, bright-eyed—
  With snowy blossoms of the May.

His Summer!   Round his bungalow
  The plantain with the palm would vie —
He was a famous soldier now—
  In tropic grace and greenery.

His Autumn!   Was it not their Spring?
  The Wattle's golden wealth of bloom—
The strong man now was mellowing—
  Was brought by children to his room.

Seasons.

His Winter! The old hero stood
  Once more beside the boughs of May :
And snow there was upon the wood,
  But then the blossoms were away.

THE TWO SPIRITS.

[Or, Optimist and Pessimist.]

Two spirits, one of Hope and one of Care,
　　Flew 'neath the self-same roof;
One's garment was of black and chill night air,
　　The other's of sun-woof.

One brought the warmth and light into the room
　　Upon the bleakest days ;
The other threw a shade of chill and gloom
　　Athwart the sun's own rays.

The spirits, she of Care and he of Hope,
　　Loved one another well,
Although no reader of the horoscope
　　Dared such a love foretell.

They clung but did not blend: the robe of dun
    Upon the back of Care
Could not be patch-worked with the woven sun,
    Which he of Hope must wear.

Now it was night; and then the star of pain
    The joyous sun outshone :
Now it was day; and in the light again
    The evil star had gone.

In some soft twilight in the latter days
    May this strange pair be dight,
Without the dazzle of the sun-robe's rays,
    Nor yet as dark as night.

THE HOUR OF PRAYER.

WHENEVER the Poet heard the hour
Chimed from the neighbouring belfry tower,
    He bowed his head to pray.
Held he that some mysterious power
    In words then uttered they?

Or was it this that the striking chime
Reminded him of the flight of time,
    And life that ebbed away,
Or church bells ringing at matin-prime,
    And noon and close of day?

He did remember some legend old,
In which were mystical virtues told
    Of pray'r at chime of hour,
And thought how swiftly life's current rolled,
    When spoke each antique tower.

And hearing hours from the belfry chime
Reminded him of the olden time,

When pious mass was sung
And bell for pray'r at each day's prime

And noon and close was rung.

Not often the Poet knelt to pray
In churches during the Sabbath day,

But while he heard the chime
Peal from the belfry, he turned alway

And gave to God the time.

Whether it was that the striking chime
Reminded him of the flight of time,

And life that ebbed away,
Or church bells ringing at matin-prime,

And noon and close of day.

A LEGEND OF THE SABBATH.

THERE is a legend old, which says
That God comes down on Sabbath days
    A little nearer earth,
And posts His angels in the ways
    To gather deeds of worth.

It did mayhap originate
In some old preacher's pious pate,
    His people to induce
One day a week to consecrate
    Unto religious use.

For, thinking God was nearer earth
And angels' questing deeds of worth,
    They sanctified this day
Alike from labour and from mirth
    To do good deeds and pray.

The legend may be true or no ;
Good men believed it long ago,
  And profited thereby,
If once a week they acted so
  As if their God was nigh.

We live in an enlightened age
And war on superstition wage,
  And yet no better do
Than those who hearing this adage
  Believed it to be true.

THE LOST POEM.

December 31st, 1884.

It was the death-night of the year;
The night was frost-begemmed and clear;
  The Poet in his study sate,
And cried, " Upon this magic night
A glittering poem will I write
  To make my name for ever great."

The Poet in his study sate
Prepared to woo his Genius late
  And watch the crowding thoughts appear,
While, echoing through the frosty air,
In clear voice should the chimes declare
  The dying moments of the year.

He watched the crowding thoughts appear,

And looked forth on the dying year,

    And saw the moon illume the trees ;

The stars were vigilant on high,

A low wind from the sea did sigh,

    And bells were borne upon the breeze.

He saw the moon illume the trees,

And heard the murmur of the seas ;

    Already seemed his Genius by ;

The nearer silence, distant bells,

Clear frost and starry sentinels

    All waked the soul of Poesy.

Already seemed his Genius by,

When Beauty with her pleading eye

    Soft-stealing to the Poet's side,

Sat on a footstool at his feet,

As richly, confidently sweet

    As though she were his wedded bride.

Soft-stealing to the Poet's side,
She wistfully his glances eyed,
　　Her face transfigured by the fire,
Her clear cheek spirit-touched, her hair
Shot-sungold in its flickering glare,
　　Her mien instinct with sweet desire.

Her face, transfigured by the fire,
Was raised to deprecate his ire ;
　　Her hands upon his knee she clasped,
And looked at him as if to say,
" Be gracious to me if you may,
　　Love's fetters on these hands are hasped."

Her hands upon his knee she clasped,
And in her thrall his soul she grasped :
　　A moment was there struggle keen,
Between the shapes that crowded round,
Waiting with language to be crowned,
　　And her—the crowned by Beauty queen.

A moment was there struggle keen,
Then the shapes vanished, for his queen
   Opened her lips—'twas but to kiss—
The ring upon her fair hand set,
As love-knot, keep-sake, amulet
   When she had promised to be his.

Opened her lips—'twas but to kiss—
When, taking both her hands in his,
   He rose beside her, with his eyes
Deep-fathoming the liquid blue,
To sound the sweet soul whence he drew
   Love in mute eloquent replies.

He rose beside her, with his eyes
Afire with love and sweet surprise,
   But with the hauntive look, which told
The seer of shapes beyond the ken
Of unitiated men,
   Already from his visage rolled,

Q

But with the hauntive look, which told
That he could mysteries unfold,
  Replaced by that ecstatic gaze,
Which says that fear nor fire nor death
Will move him, while he draws his breath,
  From the rapt worship, which he pays.

PATRIOTIC POEMS.

A LETTER FROM GORDON.

[DATED SEPT. 9th 1884—QUOTED IN THE DESPATCH FROM LORD WOLSELEY TO SIR E. BARING, DATED NOV. 29TH 1884.]

DATED the ninth of September—Khartoum—

A letter from Gordon—what had he to say?

It reads like a presage of coming doom,

" While you are all feasting and sleeping away,

With us it is nothing but watch and fight,

Both soldiers and servants, by day and night."

" Yes ! we can hold out four months—and then?

' Why our hearts are weary with this delay : '

How many times have we written for men?

How many times have ye—not said nay,

But thought not of answer to those who fight

For Egypt—aye England—by day and night.

" A handful of English,—and war will cease,

   The Arab return to his tents again,

And the fellah from here to the sea have peace ;

   If you send them not now, you must send them

      then :

A handful of English—without delay—

O ye who are feasting and sleeping all day."

   Verse 2, line 2, is a literal translation from Gordon's letter.

PRAYING FOR GORDON.

[In the Churches of England, Sunday Feb. 8th, 1885.]

PRAYING for Gordon—if in Khartoum,
  Waiting, we know, in his valiant way
At an instant's notice to meet his doom,
  A man who has walked with his God alway,
  With God for his country, who stood at bay
Forsaken in Africa far away.

Surely God would not forsake his own,
  Even though praying there had been none :
But He has promised when two or three
  Are gathered together, with them to be :
And our prayers are rising to heaven, we hope,
  But our thoughts are straying across the sea
To the handful of English sent out to cope
  With a barbarous foe in a far off land,
  Wearied with marching on burning sand,
  And weak with the wounded of Abou Klea,
  But strong in the spirit which aye has brought,
On many a doubtful and desperate day,
  The "thin red line," when it stood at bay,
  To hold the "positions," for which it fought.

But hear us, Father, while we pray

For those in peril on the land,

As thou of late heardst those who be

On land, when we were on the sea,*

Voyaging past the Red Sea coast,

Abreast of the beleaguered host,

Hear us and stretch a shielding hand

Over thy servant—if in Khartoum,

Waiting, we know, in his valiant way

At an instant's notice to meet his doom,

As ready to face his God as the fray.

---

* Written a few months after the Author's return from Australia by the Red Sea route.

GORDON IS DEAD.

GORDON is dead in Khartoum,
    Dead ere deliverance came,
Ready we know for his doom,
    Yet the disgrace is the same ;
Those, who his mission decreed,
Failed him in hour of his need.

Who is to blame for his death ?
    He whose hand opened the gate ?
He whose ball robbed him of breath ?
    No ! those who left him to fate ;
Until the voice of the land
Thundered too loud to withstand.

Toss in your timorous sleep,

    Ye, who had left him to die,

Ye and the women may weep,

    England awaits your reply.

"Where is your brother," cries she,

Answer as Cain did, will ye?

Had we no soldiers to send?

    Had we no ships on the sea?

Had we not wealth without end?

    Did ye not know what would be?

One thing we had not to spare,

Gordons, like this one, to dare.

Now we have no one to save,

    But we must fight for prestige:

Gordon, the bravest of brave,

    Could have been saved from his siege,

With but a tithe of the men,

Had they been sent to him then.

Yes ! we must fight till we win,

    Lest the old pride of our name,

Carried from Spain to Pekin,

    Lose the fresh gloss of its fame :

And the dark infidel boast,

That he has conquered our host.

" England expects " . . and our *men*

    All do their duty we know,

Heedless of " where " and of " when "—

    Once let them march on the foe ;

" England expects others too,

Statesmen their duty to do."

"ADVANCE, AUSTRALIA !"

[To the Unfederated Colonies of Australia who are
sending Troops to the Soudan.]

A sound from the shimmering towns
   On Australia's strand ;
A sound from the sheep-studded downs
   In the heart of the land ;
'Tis a sound they have heard not before,
'Tis the voice of the Spirit of War.

To hardship and peril inured
   Is the bush-pioneer,
Who thirst at its worst hath endured,
   And who dreads not the spear
Of the native who lurks in the pass,
Or the fang of the snake in the grass.

Enamoured of pleasure and ease,
   Is the dweller in town,
Of sports in the sun and the breeze,
   Till the darkness comes down,
Of dances and dreamy delight
In the balmier air of the night.

But no bushman will stay with his sheep
   On the far away downs,
And his pleasure no lounger shall keep
   In the shimmering towns
Whom Australia has summoned to go
To the war on her Motherland's foe.

O land of the vine-hidden hill
   And the wide-growing wheat,
Where only Peace lingereth still
   In the track of our feet,
We rejoice that the Spirit of Pride
In caresses of Peace hath not died.

O land of the gold garnished reef
And the sheep-studded plain,
Thou dost not forget us in grief
Or forsake us in pain :
O land of the wool and the wine,
And the corn and the gold, we are thine.

II.

An evil more deadly than war
For the free to deplore,
Is loss of the spirit which fills
Wild morasses and hills
With that feeling of home, that made bold
The Scot and the Switzer of old.

The mother of nations is she
And the friend of the free ;
Till free men have fought for one cause,
Not a legion of laws
Can an Athens or England create
Though its rulers declare it a state.

III

Go forth, O, our children, and prove
  That the peace of the skies
Which shine on the land that you love
  Hath not weakened your eyes
For the glare of the lightning which plays
Where the soldier must gather his bays.

Go forth from your east and your west,
  From your north and your south,
Be the best in the battle your best,
  Share each peril and drouth
That when back in Australia again,
You the comrades of camp may remain.

Is envy to silence her voice,
  And your empire to come?
It will be when the rivals rejoice
  Over honour brought home,
And lament over comrades in doom
Who may fall in the breach at Khartoum.

WAITING FOR WAR.

APRIL 1885.

YES, we are waiting for war,
  Not in old England alone
Swelleth the ominous roar,
  Oft in the centuries known,
But from our sons overseas
Echoes are borne on the breeze.

Thought ye the blood of the North
  Beat in our pulses no more,
The storm-loving blood which sent forth
  Rollo and William of yore,
The blood of the race who were gods,
In scorn of what men reckon odds?

II.

We slept till the Muscovite deemed

That the Berserking spirit had died,

But while we were sleeping we dreamed

Of our deeds in the days of our pride,

And now with a wrench for the rust

Our sword from its scabbard is thrust.

We've wealth for the sinews of war,

We've hunger that heroes creates,

We've waited till Patience no more

Could palter with foes at the gates,

And now we are ready to fight,

With hearts that clear conscience makes light.

III.

Yes, we are longing to fight.
    Peace, with her tortuous ways,
Robs the upright of his right,
    Lost in diplomacy's maze
Much have we been, but we know
How to hit out at a foe.

Soldier and stayer-at-home,
    Sailor and settler-abroad,
Yearn on that pathway to roam,
    Oft by our ancestors trod,
Which through the battle-field leads
Either to death or great deeds.

GORDON OF KHARTOUM.

A HERO he, born out of his due time
  In this peace-grubbing, trade and taxes age,
  A man more fit to dignify the page
Of Sophocles or glitter in the rhyme
Of him who drew Horatius—too sublime
  For Birmingham and Chelsea—fit to wage
  A war to save a people's heritage,
To lead the Scots and Switzers in their prime
  Against the great-limbed conqueror of Wales
    Or Burgundy's Bold Duke.

                To Italy,
Where pride not yet nor patriotism fails,
  Thy Mother should have borne thee to outvie
The men who built the nation, which we see,
Which has been Rome and Rome again may be.

R

TO OUR CHILDREN.

"ADVANCE Australia!"   Canada advance
   To stand beside you mother 'mid the roar
   Of battle in the desert.   Only war
Can forge a nation : Germany and France
Had to engage with all their puissance
   Ere Germany was unified once more ;
   The conquest of Granada came before`
Spain's splendour : but for Salamis perchance
   Athens had borne no story and no song :
      Great singers of great actions are the fruit,
      As witness Chaucer after Poictiers,
   And Shakspere the Armada : now, ere long,
   A nation in Australia shall root,
      An Austral Æschylus attune his lay.

ENGLAND AND ATHENS.

I.

KHARTOUM has gone : Kassala too must go
  To show the world that England, if not yet
  By statute a republic, can forget
Her allies as republics long ago,
Veered by each puff of party that might blow,
  Above, below, within, without,—have set
  An infamous example.   Great the debt
Not for her writers only, that we owe,
  To Athens.   She has taught us that a state
    Of warlike men whose greatness sprung from war,
  In commerce and free institutions great,
    May, by an Æschines beguiled, deplore
Freedom and empire lost alike while he
Rises upon the ruin of the free.

II.

Athens, an old-world queen of liberty
   Enslaved in name of Freedom ! Is not she,
   A voice from Fate to England : on the sea
Her navies swept imperial : she could vie
With the world's fleets united ; could defy
   The menace of the nations : she was free
   But lost her freedom when she came to be
Pitted against a despot-enemy
   Who met the feeble, vacillating sword
     Of men who fought for self and party first
   And commonweal and country afterward,
     With his unwavering phalanxes, that burst
   Upon the long-effete Hellenic world
   Like thunderbolts from Mount Olympus hurled.

III.

Athens and Carthage ! What high-hearted boy,
  Who reads of antique Greece and Italy
  On history's page, but breathes a generous sigh,
When Rome and Sparta triumph, thrills with joy
When Hector does a doughty deed for Troy,
  And Hannibal and Conon light the sky,
  Darkling to night, with fires of victory,
While Fate their homes advances to destroy ?
  Athens and Troy and Carthage ! We love all
    For their brief empire-splendour.   But we can
  Scarce find a sigh for Athens' second fall
    Before the youthful Macedonian
  In ardour fresh his mission to fulfil,
  While she was impotent for good or ill.

TO ENGLAND,

ON THE VERGE OF WAR WITH RUSSIA.

IMPERIAL England, have thou no alarms !
 Not if all Europe look on thee askance,
  If war be hurled by Russia, hate by France,
When, at thy first reveillée, spring to arms
Thy children unseduced by safety's charms
 In far-off isles, and those who wielded lance
  Against thee erst, unsummoned, now advance
To fight beneath thy flag in dusky swarms.
 Old Europe grimly smiles to see each whelp,
  From the bright South to frozen Labrador,
 Couching to leap across the sea to help
  The Lion, when he rolls his battle-roar,
 And hails the art of Hannibal, in those
 Who fill their armies from old Indian foes.

HEROUM FILII.

DEDICATED TO THE "SCOTS GREYS."

I.

O LET me tread in these degenerate days
　　The battle-fields where our forefathers hewed
　　The fashion of our greatness,—oft imbued
With torrents of red blood, I know, their bays,
With shrieks of anguish often blent their praise,
　　With tax and tallage, every year renewed,
　　The land too often groaning in the feud
Of feudal lords or kings' succession-frays.
　　Give us the want, the bloodshed and the tears
　　　If we may have the glory !　Poictiers
　　　　Recalls to me its triumph not its cost,
　　And Balaclava not the anxious fears
　　　Of child and wife and mother far away,
　　　　But the grey chargers ploughing through a host.

II.

Degenerate days of statesmen not of men !

From Burnabys and Beresfords to clowns

Fresh from the plough and gamins from great towns,

In heat and peril, weariness and pain,

They prove them English of the ancient strain

Who on the fields of Picardy won crowns,

And smote the Russian on Crimean Downs,

And rode with Nelson monarchs on the main.

O happy brother-Teutons, you who have

The man, the giant of the iron will

To guard the greatness of your Fatherland,

Unmoved by hate of Gaul or wile of Sclav,

And with his thunder Party's voice to still

When it is raised against the patriot's hand.

MISCELLANEOUS SONNETS.

PERICLES.

HE gave its title to the golden prime
 Of Athens, called the Age of Pericles ;
 He left a name for arts of war and peace
Scarce-rivalled in two thousand years of time ;
But not for this doth he illumine rhyme
 Above all heroes of historic Greece ;
 But that when power might pall or cares might
  cease,
He lived in love as sunny as his clime.
 Surely he was of all men happiest,
  The greatest of his country and his age,
 And privileged to pillow on the breast
  Of that most famous of Eve's family,
 Whose name is writ upon Romance's page,
  Aspasia of ambrosial memory.

MARGARET OF SCOTLAND.

There's magic in the name of Margaret,

    The sweetest sound in Scotland, though the two

    Best-worshipped Margarets she ever knew

Were English : one is saint of Scotland yet.

The other we pourtray with lashes wet

    For him her countrymen at Flodden slew,

    And found, his mail arust with autumn dew,

'Mid bishop, earl, and doughty banneret

    Upon the morrow-morning. Yet for me

        The name wakes not the Scots' kings' English queens

    Widowed by English arrows, but the glee,

        Blue eyes, and glittering hair and proud sweet miens

    Of two of Scotland's daughters—born afar

    From Tweed or Aln—'neath the southern star.

PLATONIC LOVE.

I.

I HAVE not read what Plato writ of love,

But love Platonic is it not like this,

To feel thyself with all enough of bliss

If thou canst with the one companion rove,

No matter where—alone in cool alcove

Or in a crowded room—to choose to miss

A warm caress from beauty, a rich kiss

From passion's daughter rather than remove

From this one's side, to have no care but hers,

No joy complete till she has shared it too,

To be the fondest of her worshippers,

But never think or speak of love or do

Other than brother fond of brother might,

Whom tastes as well as kindred veins unite?

II.

I have a friend—of love we never speak,—
   Love in the human meaning of the word,—
   Not that our pulses are not gaily stirred
Whene'er we meet, not that we do not seek
Our company from end to end of week,
   And when we part feel like the Eastern bird,
   Of which old ornithologists averred
That when its mate was lost it turned its beak
   Into its breast. Presence is paradise,
     And absence exile—light-of-hearts like we
Know not a hell. A pearl beyond a price
     Is it for us to roam beside the sea,
   Or on the free moors all a summer day,
   With care and every human face away.

III.

And now, sweet friend! thou wilt be here again,

　There never was a maiden whom I loved,

　Whose coming back to me so strangely moved

My being as thou movest it.　We twain

Are matched so deftly in our mind's domain :

　In all the divers places, where we roved,

　The same sights caught our fancy, and we proved

Our perfect sympathy, when we were fain

　Night after night within one room to sit,

　　As busily we worked, though scarce we spoke

　Or raised an eye, but at our note-books writ,

　　Till "Twelve" with its "to-bed" the stillness

　　　broke.

　When two in silence can together spend

　Delicious evenings, each has won a friend.

WIFE-LOVE.

I.

THAT woman should endure the pain of pains
   For any man, should spend the weary weeks
   Weighed down, half crippled, lie with hollowed
      cheeks,
And wounded long days more, ere she attains
The power for most ordinary strains
   Of household life,—that she is willing speaks
   For her devotion, more than he, who seeks
In annals of a hundred heroines, gains,
   That one in all the pride and health of youth
      Should court a bed of sickness, chance of death,
   And weeks of pain, declares the noble truth
      Of woman's love and courage, as the breath
   Of all the bards who ever sang her praise
   Could not, declaiming till the end of days.

II.

Consider her returned to health once more,
    The bright, defiant hoyden of old times,
    Who would not list to love—no not in rhymes—
And trampled victims cruelly, who wore
Her beauty as a burden, since it bore
    Its train of courtship.   See how love sublimes,
    And suffering softens !   How each comer climbs
Straight to her heart, with no more cunning lore
    Than kissing baby cheeks, or calling smiles
        To baby lips, or dwelling on the growth
    And promise of the loveliness which wiles
        All eyes towards its mother.   Wise in troth
    Was old Anacreon, when as babe he drew
    The Love-God who his shelterer overthrew.

INFANCY.

When we recall the myriad accidents
  Which babe-life threaten, marvel is it great
  That they have ever come to man's estate,
Who won great wars or carved out continents!
Napoleon, for all his regiments,
  Was once a little helpless child, whose fate
  Lay balanced in his nurse's love and hate:
A chill at Cromwell's birth had changed events,
  As Rupert could not, and his cavaliers,
    In half-a-dozen battles.   When we think
      How surfeit or starvation, heat or cold,
  Neglect, unwary diet—not for years
    But hours—will sweep the infant o'er the brink,
      The marvel is that any man grows old.

ON A DEAD INFANT.

DEAD that two brothers should not disagree !

　Poor babe ! Thy brief experience of earth

　Knew little of its beauty and its worth,

But yet thou didst fulfil a destiny,

In that thou wouldst not come 'twixt him and me.

　Ten weeks of wintry weather from thy birth,

　And then thou soaredst where there is no dearth

Of sun and southern air and sympathy.

　O may no cloud, though smaller than a hand,

　　Arise again between us, lest once more

God should from us some sacrifice demand

　　Like this, which thus untimely we deplore.

We are amenable to Providence

Although we understand not in what sense.

S

BOB.

[WRITTEN ON AN INFANT'S GRAVE IN THE TORQUAY
CEMETERY.]

THIS was the child of hope: about his birth

Fair portents shone, recorded that they might,

When he had won his name, be brought to light,

And men might read the promise of his worth

In all that heralded his dawn on Earth,

And from his cradle fame begin to write.

But after a brief sojourn took he flight

Before he knew so much as grief or mirth.

High hopes are buried underneath this stone,

Where lies a child begotten overseas,

Who never breathed in that serener zone

Where, even in the winter, cooling breeze

Is welcome to the joyous folk who fare

Free and contented in the sunny air.

TOO LATE.

Whom has it not befallen at a ball

   That some shy maid, he did not note till late

   And briefly danced with, should by some ill fate

Be she who most attracted him of all :

And so in friendships will it oft befall :

   Some one for weeks has been your constant mate,

   In day-walks and night-talks inseparate,

In all you minded, sympathetical,

   And yet the closing link of sympathy

     To make the two ends of your bond to meet

Your vigilance has cheated, till well nigh

Your intercourse's season has passed by ;

     And then you see how passingly more sweet

     This intercourse had been, if thus complete.

CATHEDRALS.

I.

You, our Cathedral who would view aright,
    Think not you saw it in the hurried look,
    Which, waiting for a train, perchance you took,
Or in one day devoted to the sight.
There is a something of the infinite
    In Gothic minsters caught, which will not brook
    A dilettanti visit ; every nook
Is rich with some religion recondite ;
    Pillar and groin and corbel and keystone
        Are eloquent.   The architect may be,
    Testing each course and column one by one,
        Some glimmer of the mystery may see,
    Or the grey dean, whose life for many a year
    As chanter, curate, canon, hath been here.

II.

Choose you to know our minster as they do?

  Go dwell beneath the shadow of its walls,

  Seek it at matins, and when even falls,

And, while the flood of music thrills it through

From porch to lady-chapel, fondly view

  The old-world carving on the canons' stalls,

  Where favoured thou mayst sit, or finials

Upon some baron's tomb, and note the hue

  Which glass took in the third King Henry's reign,

    The delicacy of the tracery

  Which held it in the windows, and rich stain

    And symbolism spent in days gone by

  Upon the rood-screen, and then, wondering,

    glance,

  Over the nave's vast pillars and expanse '

III.

So mayst thou learn, when many a chaunted psalm

  Hath risen from thy lips, and many a time

  Knee hast thou bowed beneath the roof sublime,

To know the stones not only, but the calm

And mystic atmosphere which yields the charm

  In places, where pray'r hath not ceased to climb

  Up heaven's altar-steps, and bells to chime

Summons of joy or worship or alarm

  For twenty generations. Only those

  Who spend their lifetime on it know a thing :

Who lives outside at best can say he knows

  " Of it " not " it," for all his studying :

But " knowing of " not " knowledge " must suffice

For men in daily labour's iron vice.

EXETER CATHEDRAL.

NOT greatest of our minsters is the fane
  Of Exeter, but dear it is to me
  As the first fresh one, which I chanced to see
(Though I had been to Westminster again
  And huge St Paul's) since I recrossed the main,
  From the New England in the Southern Sea,
  Where ancient minsters are not.   Royally
It rises up, with tracery, rich pane
  And sculptured niches glorious its west,
    And Norman towers its centre, and its east
    Inside with antique tomb of knight and priest,
  Rood-screen and bishop's throne.   And by me
      stands
  She whom I think of many maids the best,
  A pilgrim, like myself, from Austral lands.

COCKINGTON LANES,

NEAR TORQUAY.

RARE afternoon in an October rare !
  We passed red cliffs environing blue seas,
  Red lanes with green banks bounded and elm trees ;
The sky was clouded lightly ; soft the air
And fresh and soft the breezes ; the rich glare
  Of red and green was almost Cinghalese,
  Recalling for the traveller reveries
Of red-tiled roofs and palm-tree groves, so fair
  To unaccustomed eyes ; but soon the green
    Of elms with linden-yellow, hawthorn-red,
  And marvellous horse-chestnut-orange sheen
    Was tempered, and once more 'twas mine to tread
  The merry, crackling leaves—a sound scarce known
  In ever-green Australia's milder zone.

A WALK IN SPRING.

[FROM TORQUAY TO MARLDON.]

SPRING's many voices—cawing of the rooks,
  Bleating of lambs, the blackbird's clucking note,
  The echo from the teamster's sturdy throat,
The babble of the rain-replenished brooks.

Spring's cheerful sights—the flowers in their nooks
  In wood and bank, the fields in their new coat
  Of fresh-ploughed red, the squirrel perched remote,
The student lured by sunshine from his books.

Such hear I, such I see the day I go
  Across the hills to Marldon, snowdrops here
To light the eye, and on each fresh-ploughed row
  A parliament of rooks to greet the ear,
Until the turning road before me flings,
The grey old Church gay in five hundred springs.

DEVONSHIRE.

Broad county of deep hedge-rows and blown trees,

    With wild deer ranging on thine eastern heights,

    And salmon in thy spates, and rich in bights

And wooded estuaries and pebbled quays,

Elbowed against the western storms and seas !

    Great mother of Elizabethan Knights,

    Who fought in frozen seas and famous fights,

And bearing in thy quaint-named villages

    The impress of the Norman, as thou bearest

        The emblem of the Briton on thy moors !

Nor is this all thou boastest but the fairest

        Of mead and orchard, yielding oft-sung stores

Of cream and cider—for thy wealth with fame

As great as for wild beauty and high name.

BOWOOD.

[NEAR "BIDEFORD IN DEVON."]

A WHITE farm-house on Daddon hill's bluff crest,
  In true Devonian-wise environed round
  With deep-sunk lanes all honey-suckle-crowned,
Walled in securely from the blusterous west,
Whose wrath the trees, blown arbour-shape, confessed,
  Thou, with some ever-echoing homely sound
  Of cattle byre or barnyard, horse or hound,
My soothing refuge wer't for thought or rest
  One cloudless August through.   At sunset's hour
    A furlong from thy gateway, I could hear
  The wild wood-pigeon coo, and see the tower
    Of Abbotsham between the elm-tops peer,
  And, if the even were not overcast,
  Rough Lundy scarred with western wave and blast.

II.

Oft have I paused a moment at thy gate

    To watch the sun its seething scarlet steep

    In sea, and myriad rooks fly home to sleep,

As I returned from pilgrimages late,

From where King Hubba met with his red fate

    By men of Devon, or some ruined keep

    On Cornish headland threatening the deep,

Or little haven, now of low estate,

    But whence, in days of great Elizabeth,

        The Grenvilles, Drakes and Raleighs issued forth

    In the swift gnats of ships, which stung to death

        The Spanish monsters, when they came in wrath

    To scourge with stake and sword the little realm

    That dared to doubt their power to overwhelm.

TOR STEPS—A BRITISH BRIDGE NEAR EXMOOR.

Tor Steps,—a relic of the ancient race

    Who ruled the land, a causeway of vast stones

    Built in the days of men with giants' bones

And heroes' might,—thou standest in thy place

After Time's storms have conquered to efface

      The Celt's and Saxon's, Dane's and Norman's

        thrones.

    Who knows if thou hast heard not ringing tones

From Arthur, glowing with an Exmoor chace,

    Or rooting out some robber-prince, who made

      His fastness in the savage moorland combes,

    Or maybe with a gentle cavalcade

      Of ladies in rich silks from ancient looms?

    The bridge stands: the brown river ripples on :

    But errant-knight and tourney-queen have gone.

THE HERB-ROBERT.

[WRITTEN CLOSE TO ILSHAM FARM, TORQUAY, IN WINTER.]

HERB-ROBERT, wherefore Robin of the flowers?
  Because thou art their Red-breast, red in leaves
  And blossoms, when the latest of the sheaves
Have long been garnered and ere April showers
Have filled the womb of May and she embowers
  All Nature.   Not the glow on summer eves,
  Just ere the sea the setting sun receives,
Can shame the crimson, which in autumn hours
    Flows through thy fronds, and thy wee pink-tinged
      bloom,
    Amid the darkness of November days,
  Serves with its small light to dispel the gloom—
    Its small light hardly noticed mid the blaze
Of huge bright summer-blossoms—as sick room
  Is cheered by humble folk with kindly ways.

THE BEECH TREE.

.

[WRITTEN AFTER A DRIVE FROM BERRY POMEROY
TO TORQUAY, IN AUTUMN.]

GIVE me of all our English trees the beeches,

  Upright, smooth stemmed, and shapely in their

      spread

  Of leafy boughs, in summer raimented

In glossy green and, when November preaches

His warning to the failing year in speeches

  Of gust and frost, so gloriously red

  That all the hollows where the leaves lie dead,

Rival the glow of crimson on the peaches

  In hothouse reared.   Not for fair stem and leaves

    We praise thee only ! have we not, when boys,

    Declared thy nuts superior to the joys

  Of walnuts fenced securely ? Have not eves

  Of chilly Christmases mid London fogs

  Been transformated by thy blazing logs?

THE SONNET'S SCANTY PLOT.

I.

WHAT are the sonnet's province? Not conceits
    On trivial themes from classic fable brought,
    And tricked in phrases studiously sought
From Spenser and, his brother bee-hive, Keats,
But portraits of the spectacle which meets
    The poet's eye, when such a fight is fought
    Or such a glimpse of such a glory caught
Or when some tale of fire his fury heats.
    Sonnets should seize the floating thought or sight
        And fix it like the graphic plate which takes
    The impress of the image in the light
        And, with long pains developed after, makes
    The features or the landscape, which it scanned
    In Nature's breadth, yet truth of detail, stand.

II.

And therefore Wordsworth's sonnets do we love,
   Wholesome and hearty, simple and direct;
   He strove not after mystical effect,
Nor divers hues in patchwork interwove,
Which rival not the plumage of the dove,
   So perfect in its prism, but the specked
   And garish clothes which savages select
When the trade-schooner runs into a cove
   Of coral isles.   He tells us what he felt—
   A simple man with open sympathy—
Seeing the morning haze from London m
   Or gazing on the glorious tracery
Of " King's," or sitting by his cottage fire
A king himself for satisfied desire.

OXFORD, THE GRAND UNDOER.

I.

OXFORD, the Grand Undoer, thou dost cost

    More than thou yieldest those who tread thy stones,

    Not unforgetful of the men, whose bones

Have lain long ages in their bodies' dust

But who were once the glory and the trust

    Of college, then of country—more than once

    Of country first,—if then, as at the nonce,

The man, who academic honours lost,

    Was laying the foundations of a name

    More lasting than a roll of scholarships,

A fellowship, and medals—or the fame,

      Which halos a great teacher of the hour,

     To undergo perpetual eclipse

      Upon the rise of some new teaching power.

II.

Oxford, the Grand Undoer, thou undoest

   The men, who in their ordinary sphere

   Might have made many a hundred pounds a year

As merchants, lawyers, doctors, whom thou wooest

To this of true æsthetic lives the truest—

   The quest of knowledge free from any care

   If golden fruit or not this knowledge bear—

These, when to true disciples thou subduest,

   Thou takest from their own broad, beaten path

     To wander in the pleasaunces, where they

   Cull neither first-fruits nor the after-math,

      But only wander with an aimless pleasure,

     Losing at every hour and turn their way,

      And finding nought of the too-scanty treasure.

III

Oxford, the Grand Undoer ! he, on whom
   Thou layest the enchantment of thy rule,
   Can never settle to an office-stool
But with the feeling of a living tomb,
Or give his thoughts and industry in gloom
   Of London courts to ledger work, or school
   His mind, attuned to antique cloisters cool
In Oxford, to a hot and whirring room,
   With vast machines and hands-in-hundreds filled.
     He has lived the life of Oxford and can ne'er
The fairy castles in his brain unbuild ;
      And, though 'mid looms and ledgers he may sit,
   His heart and fancy never will be there
    But to the country of his castles flit.

IV.

Oxford, the Grand Undoer—whom indeed

   Undost thou not? The giants of their kind,

   The men who have such mastery of mind

That the world stops to listen or to read

Their pregnant words, of pregnant work the seed.

   In ordinary callings of mankind

   Such men would waste their powers, would not find

The where-withal of food their minds to feed.

   These Oxford calls from following their sheep

      To intellectual thrones. By her not found

   Their mighty intellects would eat, drink, sleep,

      And die within their sheep-folds, and the world

      Would know not of the royal heads uncrowned

      The oriflammes of genius unfurled.

V.

Oxford is not a school for little men,

But training ground, where men of giant mould

May the full powers of their frames unfold,

At best a lottery where few may gain

Aught but the paltriest prizes, or attain

To heights where they may strike a bee-line bold

Unto the goal, which in their minds they hold.

The rest must linger in the thick-scrubbed plain

Where, if they leave the common beaten track,

They lose themselves—too lucky if they can

Win by supremest efforts their way back.

Oxford is but a school for drudge and king.

For him no king, and yet no common man,

She hath but little in her hand to bring.

ADDENDA.

THE DEDICATION OF "A SUMMER CHRISTMAS."

[To Mrs George Cawston.]

To You, with whom I wandered oft,
　Ere overseas swift ship I took,
Where Ingleborough looms aloft
　Or in a Surrey orchard-nook,
　To You I dedicate this book.
For Wattle, though I sang not Oak,
　And Austral creek not English brook,
Yet English hearts love English folk.

To You beneath whose roof so oft,

    Ere overseas swift ship I took,

Upon the ball-room skirmish soft

    'Twixt brave and fair 'twas mine to look,

    To You I dedicate this book.

Though later southern beauty woke

    Chords which my deepest heartstrings shook,

Yet English hearts love English folk.

To You the friend to whom so oft,

    Ere overseas swift ship I took,

Heroes I sang on hills aloft

    And wooers in a woodland nook,

    To You I dedicate this book.

Though myths of stranger lands I spoke

    And for strange lands my own forsook,

Yet English hearts love English folk.

ENVOY.

To You I dedicate this book,
    And Wattle though I sang not Oak
And Austral creek not English brook,
    Yet English hearts love English folk.

THE STARRY SISTERS.

GLORIOUS is that which dazzles from afar,
    And mystery enthralls.   Astronomy,
    Can she with her poetic sister vie,
Who read by patient watching of a star
Not size and distance only but the war
    Of fortunes good and evil?   Do we buy,
    With knowledge which will brook no augury,
A recompense for thirst men had of yore
    In drinking from their futures?   Jupiter
        Retains his borrowed brightness, Mars his hue
        Of soldier-red, but vanished from our view
    The Horoscope and grey astrologer,
        Though from the discrowned science great men
            drew
    High inspiration in the days that were.

FORSTER'S " MIDAS."

Finished, in the rough only, on the day that the
Author the Hon. Wm. Forster, sometime Premier
of New South Wales, died.

Finished the task, but then the writer's term
   Was finished with it.   Feebly had his hand
   Writ the last words when to the shadowy land
He passed across, not with old age infirm
But having long within him borne the germ
     Of   sudden   death.   For   else   he   would   have
        scanned
Each line and word most critically, banned
Each loose idea, awkward phrase, ill form.
   But, Reader, hold it sacred what he writ,
     For hardly dry the writing when he died,
And therefore not he only uttered it
     But death within him.   Words thus sanctified
'Twere sacrilege to alter or omit ;
     As death hath ordered, so it should abide.

TO SIR SAMUEL WILSON,

OF HUGHENDEN MANOR, BUCKS, AND ERCILDOUNE,

AUSTRALIA.

OFTEN by hostile critics carped at erst
  You have lived down their censure.   Now you stand
  Known through the length and breadth of this
      great land
As one who toils for England's greatness first
Nor place and profit afterward, who durst,
  When patriot hopes were low and hearts were fanned
  By slander's breath to fury, join the band,
Of constant men that braved the wild outburst
  Of wrath and hate by fickle millions hurled.
    Yours is the steady purpose which has won
  History's giants their glory in the world :
    You proved its fibre 'neath a fiercer sun,
  Where Melbourne's hall * attests how well your will
  Tamed Austral wilds with wealth your hands to fill.

---

  * The Wilson Hall in the Melbourne University, the gift of
Sir Samuel, is the finest building in Melbourne.

TO J. HENNIKER HEATON, Esq.

AN ENTERPRISING AND SUCCESSFUL COLONIST OF NEW SOUTH
WALES, AND A MUNIFICENT CONTRIBUTOR TO THE
PATRIOTIC FUND, WITH WHICH SHE IS SUPPORTING HER
CONTINGENT TO THE SEAT OF WAR.

SMILING, stout England sees her sons go forth
   To seek their fortunes o'er the southern main :
   It proves them worthy of the ancient strain
Which sallied out to conquer from the North.
And loves she, when they've well displayed their worth,
   To hold them to her bosom once again,
   Where, if their hearts beat high, they would remain
Rather than in the softest air of earth.

   And Kent is proud of him who hewed his way
      In the new land so swiftly, who doth yet,
   Though his heart bids him in the old land stay,
      The home of his adoption not forget,
   But strains his purse to make her burden light
While she sends sons in England's ranks to fight.

PRIMROSE DAY.

'Twas only the pale little Primrose,
   The pride of a glade in the wood ;
Men gathered the blossom in April
   In the sweet of its primrosehood ;
'Twas pale and its fragrance was faint,
But 'twas free as the snowfall from taint.

'Twas only the pale little Primrose,
   Not the pride of the hothouse, they chose,
When under the blossoms of April
   The patriot passed to repose ;
'Twas humble, but all loved it well,
And took it their feelings to tell.

And England now treasures the Primrose,

    As she treasures not even her Rose ;

'Tis the emblem of National Honour,

    Of Peace, without cringing to foes ;

Thus even the wild flowers of spring

Their praise to the patriot bring.

W A R.

WHAT meaneth the hum of the dockyards, the knightly
old music of steel ?

What meaneth the hum of the city, the tramp of the
well-timed heel ?

What meaneth the banner of England from the stern
of the mail-ship swung?

What meaneth the note of defiance with the voice of
a people flung ?

WAR.

We hide not the sorrows of warfare, the widow, the
want, and the woe ;

We hide not the perils of warfare, the might of a
resolute foe ;

But our eyes are beginning to glitter as our fathers'
flashed ages ago,

When our Edwards went forth to their battles with
the men of the bill and the bow.

𝕺pinions of the 𝕻ress

OF A SUMMER CHRISTMAS.

The BRITISH QUARTERLY REVIEW, *January 1st,* 1885, *said :—*

Mr Sladen tells his story in a vigorous Hudibrastic verse, and he relieves it by stories from the lips of his friend.   He does not claim that the work is a poem, but only a novel in verse : but certainly such pieces as " Odysseus in Scheria," " San Sebastian," which is dramatic in the most exacting sense of the word—and " Sappho," which is truly lyrical, may lay claim to being poems in themselves, and, as interludes, may lay claim to communicate something of poetic character and charm to the whole.   For ourselves, we have read the latter piece with real enjoyment and appreciation of the music and delicate fancy which mark it.   Many other portions of the volume might well claim more exhaustive notice, such as we cannot now give it.   But we commend the volume to all who care for Chaucer-like presentment of character and situation, for humour and sly satire, for imagination and real power of portraiture."

And the MORNING POST, *December 22nd,* 1884.

Mr Sladen has written a great deal of verse, but his " Summer Christmas" is by far the best thing he has done yet.   The scene is laid at a sheep station in Australia, and the background is sketched in with much truth and vigour, the small animals and birds being introduced with the loving fidelity of a Prae-Raphaelite. . . . .

All the characters are well drawn and distinct, from John Cobham the Man of Kent, down to Lachlan Smith ; and the heroine Lil is a charming type of the Australian girl. . . . .

The shorter poems are far above the average, and the Homeric tales especially are full of interest.   There are few faulty rhymes, and most of the verse is very sweet, particularly in " Sappho."

From the GRAPHIC, *February 21st,* 1885.

We have derived so much pleasure from " A Summer Christmas " by Douglas B. W. Sladen (Griffith, Farran & Co.), that it seems almost ungracious to take any exception, and indeed there is little calling for other than praise.   The idea is a good one : a party of friends and relations, assembled to keep Christmas at the Antipodes, determine to emulate the heroes and heroines of the " Decameron," but the scheme resolves itself into one of their number, the Professor, being appointed story-teller in ordinary, whilst the others choose his subjects.   In this manner are introduced a series of romantic poems in various measures, though the heroic preponderates, all of them good, and some rising to a high order of merit. Mr Sladen seems to be in his element in dealing with classical subjects—we like " Helen of Sparta " and " Odysseus " best of anything in the book— but at the same time he can do good work in other directions, as witness the story of Saida and the legend of Dunmail's Raise.   In the setting of the poems the love episode of Lil and the Professor is graceful and sympathetic, though their courtship was something of the shortest.   Altogether the volume is a very pleasant one.

U

SOCIETY, *November 22nd, 1884, says* :—

As the rhyme is above the average, and the story interesting, *per se* the final result is most pleasing. The scene is laid in Australia, and the descriptive writing is in many cases excellent; indeed the author is very modest in dubbing his work simply rhyme; in many cases it rises to the height of true Poetry, and some of the stories, interspersed after the manner of "The Tales of the Wayside," are extremely graceful.

The DUNDEE ADVERTISER, *December 11th, 1884.*

The work is pleasantly written, and here and there we come upon some rather deft touches of character-painting. In the narrative itself all is pleasant, sincere, and natural, and therefore enjoyable; while the poetic stories introduced after the manner of Boccaccio are pleasing.

And the EDINBURGH COURANT, *December 19th, 1884.*

Mr Sladen's Australian Lyrics made him sure of a friendly hearing for any new work he might offer, and his "Summer Christmas," which also deals with Australian life, is worthy of the same hand. The story he tells required very little rhyme to set it off.

And the OXFORD UNIVERSITY HERALD, *January 31st, 1885.*

The Homeric Episodes, of which there are three, especially please us : they are full of the very spirit of the Greek Poet, and of what Mr Lang, in one of his Sonnets, calls the " Surge and thunder of the Odyssey."
All ungracious fault finding aside, we rise from our perusal of " A Summer Christmas " with feelings of the sincerest pleasure, and with a hearty wish to see some more of Mr Sladen's work in the same almost unworked and most interesting field.

And the DAILY FREE PRESS, *March 19th, 1885.*

The book is certainly one of high promise. Young Australia may well be proud of her rising bard, and Old England will welcome heartily the work of her wandering son.

ST STEPHEN'S REVIEW, *January 31st, 1885 says*:—
His great merit is that he has a story to tell and knows how to tell it.

And the VIGARO, *April 18th, 1885.*
We can unhesitatingly thank him for his "novel in rhyme."

And the ACADEMY, *March 21st, 1885.*
The pictures they afford of life on an Australian sheep-run are fresh and wholesome. The Author has some acute perception of character. Mr Sladen is, as we say, a fecund writer : but while he can give us fresh pictures of unfamiliar life, we shall not tire of his many books.

And the GLASGOW HERALD.
As a story, " A Summer Christmas " is interesting and enjoyable.

And the QUEEN, *February 14th, 1885.*
Will be found entertaining.

And the ANGLO-NEW-ZEALANDER, *January 16th, 1885.*
The book well pays perusal, and will no doubt be eagerly received, not only by Australians.

OF A POETRY OF EXILES.

The EUROPEAN MAIL, *February 27th*, 1885, *says:*—

The address to Australia is a really fine poem, and in many of the pieces which fill the volume are to be found force and pathos, music and thought, form and colour, to a degree that certainly elevates Mr Sladen infinitely above the giddy heads of those "minor minstrels," whom harsh and unfeeling critics like to damn effectually with the extinguishing irony of very "faint praise." Far otherwise is it, however, with Mr Sladen, whose present volume is thickly strewn with poetic beauties. . . . .

Mr Sladen has already won well-merited fame with his "Australian Lyrics," and this very timely volume will undoubtedly add to his reputation.

And the WESTMINSTER REVIEW, *October* 1884.

He has an eye for the picturesque, and reproduces the local colouring with some skill and success. His tone is manly and sensible, but his subjects are too numerous and varied, and many of them do not lend themselves to poetic treatment at all. The descriptive sonnets give a vivid picture of Australian scenery.

The ACADEMY, *of October* 11th, 1884.

Recent Verse.

The poems in this little volume are distinctly ahead of anything that the author has hitherto published. With as much freshness of subject and as much ardour of feeling as characterised previous productions, they have more variety of theme, and more of the kind of descriptive writing which we want. What Mr Sladen, as an Australian colonist, can do better than another is to give to Englishmen at home the impressions of an Englishman abroad, concerning a new country and strange habits of life. This can hardly be done through the medium of Norwegian legends or by translations from Virgil. When the tailor poet in Kingsley's well-known story begins to exercise his gift of poetry, a practical-minded friend tells him that, if he must write, he will be wise to write about something that he knows. Some of our young poets would be seriously hampered by such advice, and totally silenced by such a necessity as it implies; but Mr Sladen has the advantage of knowing something. His descriptions of Australian scenery are often vivid, and we trust they are no less faithful than pictorial.

The FEDERAL AUSTRALIAN, *May* 31st, 1884, *said:*—

Many of the short pieces are very complete, and indicate what Mr Sladen is capable of achieving. We are greatly pleased with such little poems as "The Plaint of the Prodigal Son," "Winter," and "The Poet's Message."

And THE SOUTH AUSTRALIAN CHRONICLE.

It is thoroughly racy of the soil, and evidences that Mr Sladen has not lived amid the manifold beauties of this new land of ours without deriving novel inspirations which lift above the level of the mere imitator. His poetry does not smell of the lamp: it is fresh, bright and spontaneous, qualities that display the poet's actual communings with nature in her various moods, and his deep insight into her inner meaning.

OF AUSTRALIAN LYRICS.

The LEADER, *March 5th*, 1883, *said* :—

A charming simplicity both of expression and of idea, is their prominent characteristic, as might be expected of one who can say of Longfellow—

> "Was not his simple song
> Our sample of all song?"

The themes to which he most frequently recurs are those which enable him to sing of home and family affections, of fair women and love's young dream, and to indulge in regrets for having left Old England even for "the blue of Austral skies."

The divided feeling with which Mr Sladen regards his old home and the new is fairly exhibited in "The Squire's Brother," the longest in the collection, and, in our opinion, the best of the lot. In the first part the Squire's Brother, who is a younger son, and who has been sent out to Queensland to push his fortune as a squatter, soliloquises as he sits on a three-rail fence—

> "Nell wouldn't know me, I suppose, were she to see me now
> Thus lolling in a linen blouse and bearded to the brow ;
> I didn't wear a flannel shirt when I was courting her,
> Or buck-skin pants engrained with dirt and shiny as a spur.
>
> So here I am—a pioneer, working with my own hands
> Harder than any labourer upon my brother's lands,
> Far from the haunts of gentlemen in this outlandish place ;
> I wonder if I e'er again shall see a woman's face.
>
> I couldn't stand it, but for this, that when I first came out,
> I used to see the carriages in which men drove about,
> Who tended sheep themselves of old 'neath Caledonia's rocks,
> And now were lords of wealth untold, and half a hundred flocks.
>
> I laid this unction to my heart, that, if a Scottish hind
> Could play so manfully his part, I should not be behind;
> And so I slave and stay and save, and squander nought but youth ;
> Nell sometimes writes and calls me brave, and knows but half the truth."

Part second takes us to the old hall, where we see the returned squatter gazing at the family portraits on the walls—

> "The Photo in the frame is Nell—why I gave Dick that frame,
> And doesn't the old pet look well ! I swear she's just the same
> As when I left her years ago to cross the Southern foam,
> I wonder if they've let her know that I'm expected home."

Part third introduces us to Nellie herself, standing "before a faded carte," and thus soliloquising in her turn after having seen her old lover—

> "But Charlie's very different, he's seen the real world,
> And where no white man ever went his lonely flag unfurled ;
> He went to slave and stay and save and squander nothing but youth,
> And when I said that he was brave I knew but half the truth.

For there in intermittent strife, with hostile natives waged
He spent the best years of his life in humdrum toil engaged,
Or galloping the live long day under a Queensland sun
After some bullocks gone astray or stolen off the run.

He's handsomer, I think, to-day, although he is so brown,
And though his hair is tinged with grey and thin upon the crown,
Than in the days when he was known at "White's" as Cupid Forte,
And in good looks could hold his own with any man at court,

Well, he has come and asked again that which he came to ask
The night before he crossed the main upon his uphill task.
I answer'd as I answer'd then but with a lighter heart.
Who knew if we should meet again the day we had to part!"

And then in the fourth and concluding part we have one of those dainty
pictures which Mr Sladen paints so deftly with a few touches of his pen—a
picture of Charlie and Nellie in the first flush of married life—

"'Neath a verandah in Toorak I sit this summer morn,
While from the garden at the back, upon the breezes borne,
There floats a subtle, faint perfume of oleander bow'rs
And broad magnolias in bloom, and opening orange flow'rs,

A lady 'mid the flowers I see, moving with footsteps light,
And when she stoops she shows to me a slipper slim and bright,
An ankle stocking'd in black silk and rounded as a palm,
Her dress is of the hue of milk and making of madame.

I wonder is that garden hat intended to conceal,
All but that heavy auburn plait, or merely to reveal
Enough to make one long to catch a glimpse of what is there
To see if eye and feature match the glory of the hair.

From the FEDERAL AUSTRALIAN, *March 29th*, 1885.

He has it in him to become an Australian Longfellow ; but in order to
attain this pitch of eminence, he must become as painstaking and artistic a
worker as was the author of the "Voices of the Night."

From the MELBOURNE REVIEW, *April* 1883.

However in spite of the many, the very many blemishes, which mar the
book, there is here and there something to praise. The ode to Queen
Victoria is distinctly good, and pleases the student of Horace by an agree-
able echo of that wonderful master.

From the GRAPHIC, *July 20th*, 1883.

A true note of song is sounded from the Antipodes in "Australian Lyrics."
The pieces have all, it seems, appeared in the columns of the Colonial press,
and we can only say that any editor was lucky who could secure such a
contributor of verse. The best thing in the volume is undoubtedly "The
Squire's Brother," a tale of true love told in ringing measure, but there is
much more that will delight the lover of genuine poetry. "Mrs Watson"
is an excellent tribute to the memory of a brave, good woman, and
"Solomon's Prayer" is terse and effective. Altogether Mr Sladen's muse
is one worthy of being cultivated.

OF "FRITHJOF AND INGEBJORG, AND OTHER POEMS."

The ARGUS, *writing in the fall of* 1881, *says:*—

A further instalment of Mr Sladen's metrical version of a saga of "Frithjof and Ingebjorg" confirms the favourable opinion we expressed of the first part. It is so good both in form and substance as to justify the expectation that the writer will hereafter make his mark in the poetical literature of Australia.

And the AGE *and* LEADER, *October* 1882.

The legend ("Frithjof and Ingebjorg") is treated with artistic feeling, and the verse flows smoothly and sweetly throughout. One might even say that it proves its author to be a worthy scholar of the master who gave us the "Tales of a Wayside Inn," and express a hope that he may never fall below this achievement in future.

And the FEDERAL AUSTRALIAN, *October 19th*, 1882.

We have read the volume with pleasure, and gladly bring it under the notice of our readers, not only because it is the work of a colonist, but also because it contains much that is really good, and holds out the promise of some better work in the future. In his "epilogue" the author writes thus modestly :—

> "Australia sends this book of song
>   To England, not so much in hope
> That it will take its place among
>   The brotherhood of wider scope,
> But rather that it will be read
>   By those who take this volume up
> Remembering where it was bred.
>   We cannot, in our youth, compare
> With the full-grown and perfected
>   Poesy reared in English air."

And then, further on :—

> "Where this small sheaf of rhyme did grow,
>   We have not yet lived fifty years ;
> But as the swift hours onward flow,
>   We too shall breed poetic peers
> For Arnold and for Tennyson."

Such are Mr Sladen's high hopes, and we doubt not their realization in the not far distant future.

And the S. A. REGISTER, *and* ADELAIDE OBSERVER, *October* 1882.

Of these, "Frithjof and Ingebjorg," a Norwegian legend, written in an attempt at the old rugged style of the saga, is perhaps the best. It is too long to quote, but not too lengthy to read. There are some original ideas in it, and the language in which it is clothed is poetical. The "Squire's Brother" is also a piece in which the author has shown originality of thought, as well as skill in working out.

From the QUEENSLANDER, *December 23rd,* 1882.

The title of Mr Douglas B. W. Sladen's book is, to our Southern ears, the least musical portion of it ; but before the poem " Frithjof and Ingebjorg " has been fully perused, the reader will probably have forgotten the title and become absorbed in the romantic story cleverly woven into verse.

In " Waterloo " there is a facility of rhythm which we miss in almost every other poem. It is written in a fine inspiriting strain, which so lifts the reader up, until, to use Shelley's words—

> "The dead air seems alive
> With the clash of clanging wheels,
> And the tramp of horses' heels."

The lines are pretty well known to those who take an interest in the new literature of the colonies, and have passed from journal to journal in our small literary world with almost the same universal publication as did " Hands all Round," but with far better appreciation. There is a joyous ring in the lines—

> "On, on,
> Life Guard and Dragoon,
> An English charge and a red right hand
> Will bring fair years to your fair old land :
> With riven corslet and shivered lance
> Is reft and shivered the pride of France."

And, again, there is a charming expression in the concluding verse—

> "'Ah ! me,
> Life is sad,' said she,
> 'When the sun and sheen of it are gone,'
> And ' One loving heart is very lone ;'
> And ' Oh ! if I might lie by you
> In your soldier grave at Waterloo."

The SCOTSMAN (*Edinburgh*), *November* 30*th,* 1882, *said* :—

Mr Sladen announces himself on his title-page as "an Australian colonist," and many of his poems are on themes connected with his voluntary exile, its pleasures and its penalties, loving recollections of the old country, hope and pride in the new one. Then he has pleasant lyrics and ballads, songs of the affections, and fragments on subjects borrowed from classic story. All alike are characterised by a satisfying mastery of form and metre, a clearness and directness of style in wholesome contrast to the morbid mysticism which pervades so much the poetry of the day, breadth and elevation of thought, and a genuine appreciation of the true and the beautiful. There is nothing in the volume that the reader could readily spare; there is much that will be read again and again with hearty enjoyment.

And the GRAPHIC, *November* 1882.

There is some good verse in " Frithjof and Ingebjorg, and other Poems," The author, now resident in Australia, has something of the true poetic feeling ; it seems a pity that he has not more fully developed the vein of innate humour manifested in " My Aunt." " The Squire's Brother " is good, with a natural pathos ; " The last of the Britons " also has merit.

And the Glasgow Herald, *December 2nd*, 1882.

In the epilogue to this little collection of poems the author pleads thus or a kindly hearing :—

> " You must not judge this book of rhyme
>   By standard of the full-grown muse
> Of our good Queen Victoria's time,
>   But first in dusty tomes peruse
> The rude verse of King Edward's reign,
>   When English first came into use."

The pleading is so graceful that we are glad Mr Sladen has added it ; but there is so much beauty both of thought and language in his poems that they require no advocacy. The chief poem, which gives its name to the collection, is founded upon an old Norse Saga, some passages of which have been translated by Longfellow. But Mr Sladen is no translator. He has taken the story, and, putting it into flowing and musical verse, has shown us lovely pictures of crag and forest, blossom and bush. These are so closely entwined, one with the other, that it is not possible to separate them for quotation. Still less can we pick out any of those passages which tell in a very noble way of the struggles of the two lovers against almost overwhelming temptation ; or of the unselfish love of the aged king for his fair young bride. Even in the rough hexameters of the American poet the story is full of pathos and dignity ; but when wedded to Mr Sladen's tender and musical words, it must charm all who read it. Besides " Frithjof," there are several other long poems, which contain many beautiful passages, and there are a number of shorter pieces. Of these, " Waterloo" and " Wiltshire" are pathetic and suggestive, but they are too long for quotation. We prefer to give a few verses of " The Squire's Brother." The elder brother is " squire," the younger goes to Australia, where he works

> " Harder than any labourer upon my brother's lands,"

and wonders that " Nell" would think of him, did she see him, once the " Cupid " forte of " White's,"

> " Lolling in a linen blouse, and bearded to the brow."

He then goes on—

> " Do you suppose that old Sir Hugh, who won your lands in mail,
> Showed half the valour that I do in sitting on this rail?
> He tilted in his lordly way, and stoutly, I confess,
> But I stand sentry all the day against the wilderness.
> There isn't much poetical about an old tweed suit,
> And nothing chivalrous at all about a cowhide boot :
> Yet oft beneath a bushman's breast there lurks a knightly soul,
> And bushmen's feet have often pressed towards a gallant goal.
> And so I slave and stay and save, and squander nought but youth ;
> And if Nell said that I was brave, she only told the truth."

From the Westminster Review, *January* 1883.

We read with pleasure the tale of " Frithjof and Ingebjorg," and can recommend it to our readers. A good tale well told justifies publication.